Lucky to be Yours

SHANNON O'CONNOR

Copyright © 2023 Shannon O'Connor
All rights reserved.

All rights reserved. No part of this publication may be reproduced, distributed, or transmitted in any form or by any means, except in the case of brief quotations embodied in critical reviews and articles.

Any resemblance to persons alive or dead is purely coincidental.

Cover by M Leigh Morhaime of Lost Marbles Designs.

Character Designs by Qamber Emporium.

Edited by Beth Hale of Magnolia Author Services.

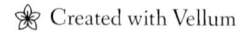

❦ Created with Vellum

Lucky To Be Yours

SHANNON O'CONNOR

Lucky To be Yours Playlist

Playlist

The Subway Song - Delacey

Can I Get Your Number - Ann-Marie

Cherry - FLETCHER & Hayley Kiyoko

talk me out of it - Olivia Holt

About Damn Time - Lizzo

Santeria - Sublime

Life Was Easier When I Only Cared About Me - Bad Suns

Radar - Britney Spears

She Said - FLETCHER

Girls Make Me Wanna Die - The Aces

I F*cking Love You - Zolita

muse - MisterWives

Chapter 1

Ellie

"We're doing green jello shots and you're going to like it," I tell Morgan and Bella. My two best friends and other halves.

"But," Bella opens her mouth while Morgan shrugs and picks up the shot.

"I don't have class tomorrow and Noel's with his dad all weekend. I just can't be too drunk when my girlfriend shows up," Morgan explains. Her girlfriend is a certifiable MILF. With the cutest eight year old and nicest ass I've ever seen. Morgan's girlfriend, not the kid. I'm a little too tipsy to be explaining things but that's what happens when you find out the woman you secretly love is seeing someone.

"I think I might be hanging out with Dylan later," Bella says like it's not soul crushing to me.

But it's not like she knows, because hell if she did I don't know if we could still be friends. So I keep my feelings to myself, and Morgan who shoots me a quick 'you good?' look, and I pretend I'm fine. Which is why I'm suggesting jello shots at 10am like we're in some kind of a frat. But it's also St. Patrick's Day, the day of my people and I plan on getting shitfaced.

"Is she joining us for the parade?" Morgan asks. We always catch the end of the parade by the time we're on our way to another bar.

"I'm not sure, she might if Lucy goes." Bella takes her shot with a cute little wrinkle of her cheeks and shrugs. Lucy, Morgan's girlfriend with the nice ass, is best friends and co workers with Bella's I guess girlfriend. I don't pay attention enough to know what is going on between them.

"We should get changed if we want to start the bar crawl," I say, changing the subject. I am glad my friends both found someone to be with. Morgan more than Bella, but I also don't want it to be all that we talk about tonight.

My friends nod and I head into Morgan's cramped bathroom to change into my *Kiss me I'm Irish* green tee and my favorite pair of ripped jeans. My long, pink hair is curled down to my waist and my makeup is already done. I knew there wouldn't be too much time after I got to Morgan's house and I like to start things on time. Not that there is an actual schedule, but more of a list of bars we like to hit on St. Paddy's Day.

Once we're dressed, I insist we take some photos to commemorate the occasion. Bella complains as usual, someone so beautiful but hates taking photos. It is ironic.

"You're beautiful, shush and smile," I insist. She flashes me her perfectly white teeth and closes her eyes. I snap away, Morgan and I making silly faces too. It is enough for now, we'll have the rest of the day to get photos, but our makeup never looks as good as it does in the beginning of the day.

"Where to first?" Morgan asks as we leave the apartment.

"Puzzles, it's a classic and they're doing green beer specials." It is one of my personal favorite bars in the city. The owners, Sawyer and Cody, are cool as hell and it is a vibey place to hang out, especially on St. Patrick's day.

"Thank god, I love it there." Bella smiles. Oh yeah, and it might be one of Bella's favorite bars. But that is just a small bonus. Not at all why I chose to go there first.

Morgan shoots me a knowing look but I avoid eye contact. I know my crush is pointless, but it's not like I can help it. Of course finding someone to distract me today will be my objective. Even a few minutes of bliss is worth not feeling this crushing weight of loving someone who will never love you back.

We head to the subway, it's overcrowded with an array of green covered people headed to the parade or bar hopping like us. I love how New Yorkers come together for the holidays and really go all out. There is a redhead dressed as an actual leprechaun and his girlfriend dressed as a pot of gold. It is equally cheesy and adorable. I hang on to the overhead pole, knowing I have a pocketful of hand sanitizer waiting for me at the end of this trip. The train stops short and Bella stumbles into me, the weight of her petite body brushing into mine. I catch her, steadying her, and she grabs back on to the pole, blushing at her embarrassment.

"I'm so sorry," she apologizes.

"Don't worry about it." I smile. It is a hazard of

riding the subway. But I hate how good it felt to hold her, even just for a second. I need to stop having these thoughts. They aren't *"friendly"* thoughts.

"El? This is our stop right?" Morgan pokes my shoulder as the doors open, and I snap back into reality.

"Yes!" I grab my friends' hands and we jump out of the subway just before the doors shut. They really should allow more than fifteen seconds between stops.

We head down the block and Puzzles is full of people. There's a short line outside but Sawyer had said she'd put us on the list so we wouldn't have to wait. It is one of the perks of being a regular at several New York bars. I had gotten us on the list for days like today.

"Hey!" Some people complain as we tell the bouncer our names and he lets us through. I fluff my cotton candy hair over my shoulder and strut inside like I own the place.

It is the most crowded I've ever seen the place. People in a sea of green, holding green cocktails and beers while the DJ plays music on one end of the bar. All the tables are gone and there are only seats at the actual bar. We make our way through the sea of people, Bella holding on to my hand so she doesn't get lost in the crowds.

Cody's behind the bar, his shaggy blonde hair pulled into a tight man bun, donning a green t-shirt that says *'don't kiss the bartender'*, I have to imagine that was his girlfriend's, Luna's idea. He's slinging out cocktails faster than anyone else bartending, but he'd also been doing this the longest. Eventually he spots me and smiles.

"I'd say Strawberry Margarita but you probably

want something green today?" He chuckles remembering my usual order.

"Yes please, whatever's good and fruity to get me drunk. We'll have three." I point to Morgan and Bella. He nods and takes out three glasses, shaking and concocting a green cocktail for us. I hand him a credit card and ask him to start a tab.

"Here ya go." I hand them each a glass and we clink glasses.

"So how's your job going?" Morgan asks me, and I sigh. As much as I love working for Kira, lately it is starting to take its toll on me. I didn't get a job in the fashion industry to be someone's assistant, I came here to make my own line someday.

"It's fine..." I say.

"You hate it, don't you?" Bella says knowingly.

"I don't *hate* it. I just wish I could be working on my own designs instead of getting people drinks and fabric," I admit.

"Well, it's one of those things where you pay your dues now and then one day someone is getting you coffee, right?" Morgan reminds me.

"Yeah, I just wish that time was now." I take a long sip of my drink. I can't tell exactly what it is, but it is fruity, and it tastes delicious.

"How's Noel?" I ask Morgan about her sort of step son. Despite not being married, or even engaged yet, Morgan and Lucy are destined to be together.

"He's good, I miss living there but I know moving out was the right choice. Plus I see them almost every weekend anyway."

"You're almost done with classes now, right?" Bella asks.

"Yup, I graduate in May. Thank goodness. I'm so tired of the commuting upstate three times a week." She sighs, sipping her drink.

"Well, enough life talk. Let's down these drinks and go do some dancing. We need to bring the vibe back up," I decide.

"I don't know," Bella says hesitantly.

"Come on." Morgan smiles.

"It'll be fun!" I push. Bella nods and downs her drink in one continuous sip.

"Let's go!" I grab their arms and lead them past the bar and to the dance floor.

The beat drops and we start dancing as a new song comes on. I don't want to get too sweaty at the first bar, but we can't not dance. I am just thankful it is music from the current era and not Irish music or bagpipes like some bars like to play. I hate bagpipes with every fiber of my being, something about the sound is like nails on a chalkboard to my ears. I specifically picked bars that would only be playing music, not noise.

"That blonde is checking you out!" Morgan calls, leaning in to my ear. I glance over my shoulder and smile at the thin blonde with lots of tattoos that's smiling at me. She is cute but she isn't really my type.

I just shrug and Morgan drops it. I know she means well, but it is hard to check out other women when the most beautiful woman is dancing right in front of me. No. Fuck. I need to stop thinking like that. My crush on Bella is never going to happen and I know what I need to do to try and get it out of my system.

And that's when I see her, my next target. The raven haired bombshell in the motorcycle jacket across the bar.

Chapter 2

Reese

I'm not someone who believes in fate and romance and all that happily ever after crap. I'm not a skeptic, I've just lived through too many bad relationships to see the end isn't always positive. Hell, neither is the middle. The beginnings seem to be the only part that have some positives which is why I've had my fair share of flings lately. It is easier to find a woman, take her home, and never call her again than it is to have anything real. I probably sound like a fuck boy and that's fine, I wear the label proudly, although sexist. Sometimes the best things have to end before they truly begin to appreciate them.

"Are you even listening?" my friend, Mitchell, asks knowing very well, I wasn't.

"Nope, I was thinking about which girl I'm going to bless with coming home today." I smirk. Mitchell and I have been best friends since diapers and are inseparable. Our parents always thought we'd end up together if it weren't for the fact that we're both incredibly gay.

"Only one? Is it a slow day?" he teases, rolling his

dark eyes. He is a handsome guy as far as guys go. He has square rimmed glasses and a jawline to die for but he is shy as can be which doesn't help him much when it comes to meeting guys. Which is where I usually come in to save the day.

"Hey, I'm classy. I might make out with a few but I only take one girl home a day." I laugh. There is a lot of fun in kissing girls, especially girls there is no future with. *I mean why not try them all?*

"You're something, definitely not classy though." He laughs.

"So what were you saying?" I ask, remembering he asked something. I think it had to do with the guy across the bar but I can't be sure.

"The guy, the cute one. Do you think he's looking at me?" He glances over, trying to be inconspicuous, but I make it completely obvious where I'm looking.

"Don't be so obvious!" Mitchell squeals, smacking my shoulder.

"Ow." I rub where he hit. "He's looking more at his drink than anything, but the guy next to him is definitely checking you out."

"What? No, he's even cuter." Mitchell gasps.

"Exactly, so let's go over there," I urge. I am always trying to get him laid, or at least a date whenever I can. I want to get him out of his shell, he is a good guy who deserves other guys to see that.

"Are you joking? No freaking way!" His eyes widen, and I chuckle.

"Come on!" I pull his arm over before he has a chance to really protest, and we walk over toward the guys. He chugs down his green beer on the way and I smile, introducing myself to the guys.

Lucky to be Yours

"I'm Reese, this is my best friend Mitchell. We were hoping you could settle a bet between us." I smirk.

"Oh yeah? And what would that be?" the less attractive, blonde guy asks.

"Which one of us were you guys checking out?"

"Well, I was definitely checking you out, baby," the blonde guy says to me. This poor guy, I'd have to let him down gently.

"And you?" I prompt the other guy, but his answer is clear by the way he is staring at Mitchell.

"Your friend is very handsome," he says with a smile. "I'm Adam." He holds out his hand to Mitchell, who looks panicked but thankfully remembers how to shake hands.

"Mitchell." And my work here is done. Except for Blondie staring at me.

"Sorry to inform you, I'm incredibly gay." I pat his shoulder and he frowns.

"Damn, well you're still beautiful." Wow. A man who can take a rejection, *that is rare*.

"We're headed to another party but can he give you his number?" I interject, wing manning between Adam and Mitchell.

"I'd love that." Adam smiles and pulls out his phone while Mitchell does the same.

"Nice to meet you both, but we better get going." I smile and usher Mitchell out. We could've stayed for longer, we are on our own schedule, but it seems like the best play to get him Adam's number. Besides there is something about being mysterious with someone you just met to keep them thinking about you.

"Wow, I am always in awe of you working your magic, even when it isn't for you." Mitchell smiles as we leave. The cool March air hits us, and I wrap my motorcycle jacket around me.

"It's a gift," I say with a shrug. I love being able to help my friends get who they want, even if it is for more than a one night stand. As long as they are happy.

"Well, once in a while you should put it to good use." I know what he is saying. He doesn't exactly approve of my one night stand mentality and I don't blame him. There was a time where I thought I was cut out for marriage and monogamy, but that time has long passed. It will take a miracle to make me ever think differently.

"Where are we headed next?" Mitchell asks curiously.

"I told my friend Sawyer I'd stop in at Puzzles. I haven't seen her in a bit."

"Okay." Mitchell nods. It's not his first time being there. It's a different kind of bar, somewhat of a club mixed in. During the day it is usually a restaurant but for the holiday they have opened the space to let people dance and mingle.

We walk a few blocks in the cool breeze, thankful it's not snowing or we'd be freezing. Sawyer left my name and a plus one on the list, so we get in with no issues. The bar is a little more green than I like, but I know it's just for the holiday. Even the bartenders are dressed in green t-shirts and the drinks seem to be different hues of green. It is a bit of an overkill, but I know Sawyer isn't big on it either. She has to be marketing for the masses, doing what is good for business. I mean I work at Starbucks for crying out loud so it doesn't get anymore corporate America than that.

I look around for Sawyer but only find her co-owner

Lucky to be Yours

instead. I've only met him once so I don't think he'll recognize me, and when I walk up to him asking to see Sawyer he gives me a funny look.

"What can I do for you? Is something wrong?" he asks.

"No, I'm just looking for Sawyer because we're friends," I explain.

"Oh." He pauses then picks up the bar phone and makes a call. "There's a woman here to see you, uh, hold on." He looks at me. "What's your name?"

"Reese."

"Reese," he says back and Sawyer must hang up because he looks at the phone confused.

"Hey!" Sawyer comes out a moment later with a big smile on her face. We don't hug because that's way too much touching for both of us, but we smile and she touches my arm gently.

"I told you I'd stop by." I smile. "You remember Mitchell?"

"Of course." She nods, but I can tell she's thankful for the reintroduction.

"Where's that fiancé of yours? I still haven't met her. I'd almost think you were keeping her away on purpose," I tease Sawyer. She is someone who's seen my magic firsthand in this bar so I don't blame her for keeping her female fiancé away from me. Not that I'd ever make a move, but I'd probably still flirt a little bit.

"I definitely am, last thing I need is you two meeting." She chuckles. "Shit, I'm being paged. Have fun, drink, I'll try to see you later."

"See you later." I say goodbye.

"She's hot, you two ever?" Mitchell asks once she's out of earshot.

"Nah, she and I have only ever been friends. She's been seeing her fiancé for a while now," I explain and he nods.

"Well, you got me that hot guy's number. So now it's your turn."

"Not like I need the assist," I say with a smirk.

"Someone's on their game today," he says with a chuckle.

"When aren't I?" I smile at the brunette across the bar, she's dancing with her friend but making eyes at me. I sip my beer and walk over to her.

"Hey." I flash my teeth and sharp jawline that I know works wonders for me.

"H-Hi." She is nervous. Sometimes this is too easy.

"Wanna get out of here?" I lean in and whisper in her ear. Her face changes dramatically, and she splashes the drink I didn't even know she was holding in my face.

"I'll take that as a no." I clench my jaw and turn around. Mitchell's holding back laughter while he hands me a napkin.

"That did not go as expected."

"I can see that." I wipe off my t-shirt, thankful it's black. In a few minutes the stain will be gone, but I'll smell like beer for the rest of the day now.

"What did you say to her?"

"I asked her to come back with me, that one always has mixed results." I shrug. It is a gamble that usually works in my favor.

"Let's go grab a spot at those tables. My feet are killing me from all the waking we've done already today." Mitchell points to the two tables across the room, almost hidden by the crowds of people.

Lucky to be Yours

I nod and we make our way over, thankful no one beat us to them. We sit at the hightop table on the wooden barstools and place our drinks on the table. I glance around the room, looking for another woman to talk to. I am in the mood to fuck someone in the bathroom and I just need to find the right girl for that. There is something hot as hell about a woman moaning and knowing everyone nearby can hear. I've had my fair share of bathroom hookups but never in Puzzles.

Mitchell starts texting, and I can see him about to send a text to Adam. Before he can protest, I snatch his phone out of his hand and slip it in my pocket.

"You'll thank me tomorrow." I can't tell if he is drunk already or just lonely. Either way I'm not going to let him ruin the start of a new thing by coming on too strong.

"Hmf, fine." He scowls at me and sips his drink, looking around the room.

"I don't see anyone, well not anyone interesting at least." I sigh. Sometimes going out is a bust. I can easily find someone boring and take them back to my place but I like a challenge, or to find someone interesting.

"I love her hair." Mitchell smiles pointing to the door and that's when I see her for the first time.

She's beautiful, with thick delicious curves on display in tight ripped jeans and a crop top that shows off her belly. Whoever says thick girls can't wear crop tops isn't looking at this goddess. Her pink hair flows down her full breasts and I'm biting my bottom lip just thinking about what's underneath. She is heading this way and with each step I can see her gentle jiggles. What I'd do to have her sit on my face. The things I want to do to this woman are indescribable to anyone else, but hopefully she'll be down. From the way she is looking at me, she seems to be headed my way. It is nice, for once I won't have to make the first move. I love a confident woman.

"Hey." She stops right at the table with a pearly white smile.

"Hi." I smirk, straightening up on my chair a bit. This is the woman I've been waiting for.

"I'm Ellie, these are my friends, Bella and Morgan." She introduces the brunettes next to her, but I hadn't even glanced their way. I give them a quick smile and put my attention back on Ellie. I wonder if that is short for something. Ellie commands all the attention in the room, it is captivating.

"I'm Mitchell," Mitchell says a moment later, and I forgot he was even sitting there.

"I'm Reese." I hold out my hand and she shakes it with her fully green manicured hand. But I notice her two shorter nails and hold back a chuckle. There goes wondering if she is into girls.

"I love your hair," Mitchell says, looking at Ellie.

"It's cool," I add. Even though all I want to do was run my fingers through it and pull it, if she is into that.

"Thanks, I have a friend who does it." She runs her fingers through it absently.

"Did you guys want to join us? We don't really have anymore seats but I'm happy to get up," I say to Ellie and her friends.

"We were actually about to dance," one of the brunettes say.

"El?" The other brunette looks at Ellie, but she's still eyeing me.

"I'd love to dance, if you guys want the company,"

Mitchell asks, and the girls nod. Ellie and the girls exchange a quick look, and they lead Mitchell across the dance floor. Far enough where they can't hear us, but close enough where they can still see Ellie.

"Did you want to sit?" I ask, pointing to Mitchell's empty seat.

"Sure." She plops down lightly on the seat and smiles at me. A light blush creeps across her cheeks as I bite my bottom lip looking at her.

"So where's your green?" she asks, raising an eyebrow.

"Excuse me?"

"It's St. Patrick's Day and you're not wearing any green. You know what that means."

"I actually don't." I chuckle nervously.

"You get pinched." She laughs and reaches out to lightly pinch my side. I pretend it hurts but laugh along with her.

"Did you need a drink?" I ask her, changing the subject.

"No thanks, I just grabbed one of those green drinks. Not sure what was in it but it was amazing." She laughs. It's light and airy. It's incredibly loud in here, so I lean in a little bit closer to hear her.

"Sorry, it's so loud in here," I explain, closing the distance between us.

She nods before looking at my lips. Her light blue eyes getting darker with desire as that blush turns her face darker than her hair. Ellie leans in just a bit closer and I can feel the tension between us. She wants this just as much as I do. I push her pink ringlets out of the way, letting them fall to her back so I can see her better.

"You're so sexy," I murmur just loud enough for her to hear.

"Have you seen yourself?" She laughs. Her pink lips form a straight line and just as I'm going to ask her what's on her mind, her lips meet mine. She is kissing me before I even have a chance to use one of my lines on her. I open my mouth enough for her to slip her tongue inside and she smiles against me as we kiss.

Chapter 3

Ellie

I close the small distance between Reese and I. I am bold, but never this bold. Something about this woman makes me want to be even bolder than normal. She makes me nervous in a good way. There is amazing sexual tension, and if this kiss is an indication of anything, we'll have amazing sexual chemistry as well.

Her tongue slips in my mouth and I can't help but smile, that is usually my move. Our tongues dance together, lightly playing each other for dominance. Reese's hand slips down my waist and pulls me toward her, me almost falling off the stool.

"Shit, I'm sorry." She pulls back and apologizes. Realizing what she almost did.

"No worries." I shrug. But I can feel my cheeks burning up with desire. We were so into it that I forgot we aren't alone. I can feel my friends eyes on me but I don't look up. I am embarrassed. And the last thing I want to do is see Bella right now and have my feelings for her getting in the way of what seems to be a great hookup.

"Do you wanna get out of here?" she asks before I can, and I laugh.

"I was just about to ask you that."

"Perfect, I know a spot." She takes my hand and I ignore how nice it feels to be holding someone's hand. I can't recall the last time I just held hands with someone I wasn't going down on.

Reese leads me down the back of the bar, toward the bathrooms, and pushes the bathroom door open. She lets go of my hand, I assume just in case anyone else is in there. She glances under the stall doors and gives me a smile, pulling me into one of the larger stalls.

"This work?" she asks, smirking.

"Fine by me." I shrug. I've had my fair share of bathroom hookups in bathrooms not as nice as this one.

"Perfect." She locks the door and our lips meet again. Our tongues doing all the work as her hands are on my breasts in an instant. I pull her in by the belt loops on her jeans, and her tiny waist is pressed against mine.

Reese's hand slides over my stomach, reaching for my breasts under my shirt. She plays with the lace of my bralette for a moment before pushing it to the side and taking my nipple in her mouth. I moan quietly as she takes the other between her thumb and pointer finger. Biting my bottom lip, I paw at her chest, pushing her motorcycle jacket out of the way.

"Here, let me." Reese pulls it off and stops touching me just long enough to hang it on the hook on the back of the door. She's wearing a black t-shirt under that smells a bit like beer, but she's kissing me again before I can comment on it.

Her hands are on the buttons on my jeans, unhooking them with one hand and using the other hand to palm my breast. Thankfully I am wearing cute panties, they are green lace ones to go with the theme of the day. Then again, it isn't like I didn't know I'd hookup with someone at the bars. I have a habit of taking someone home, especially on the days Bella comes out with us. It is easier to go home with a stranger than to think about how I can't be with her. Fuck. Why am I thinking about her? Especially right now? She has a way of invading every inch of my mind. Even when I don't want her to. I'm trying to focus on the moment when Reese slides two fingers inside my core.

Yup, that brings me back to the moment at hand. Literally. *Fuck*. Reese's fingers are long enough to hit the right spot every time. She curls them inside me and I gasp, falling forward into her.

"Shhh, babe," she whispers.

"Mmm, fuck," I whisper back. She winks and continues pumping her fingers, getting me nice and wet. Before I know it she's pulling them out and pushing me against a wall. Reese uses one hand on my throat, the other to tug down my jeans to the floor. I'm about to ask what she's doing when my panties fall to my ankles and her mouth is on my core.

She isn't here to mess around. Her tongue finds my clit and I'm holding on to the wall to steady myself. She starts off with slow licks, but quickly picks up the pace. I can't help myself, I'm moaning and gasping out with each flick of her perfect tongue. I am usually the more dominant one so I'm not used to being taken care of like this. But I like it, *a lot*.

Reese puts her fingers back in while keeping her tongue on me, and my hips buck forward. I grab a fistful of her short, dark hair and push her closer to me. I am so fucking close and I don't want her to stop. With each pump of her fingers, she brings me closer and closer to the brink. I'm about to scream out her name when we hear the door to the bathroom open. I figure Reese will stop, or at least stand up.

"I can't believe Jeremy isn't coming!" one girl complains.

"I know! He said you guys weren't exclusive but he should still see you on the major holidays!" another girl agrees. I have no idea what they are saying nor do I care, because Reese decides not to stop fucking me. The other girls must be at the mirror because thankfully I can't hear anyone going pee, but I can hear them chit chatting.

Reese's tongue flicks my clit over and over, and I'm still just as close that when she moves her fingers inside me, I can't help myself. "Oh my gosh!" I scream before slapping a hand over my mouth. The whole bathroom goes quiet except for Reese who doesn't let up, letting me ride out my orgasm in embarrassment.

I hear the women leave the bathroom and Reese stands up smiling. She wipes the corner of her mouth with two fingers and stands up to kiss me. Something about kissing after sex is hot as hell to me. I can taste myself on her lips and it is something that drives me wilder than it should. I tug back on my panties and jeans, buttoning them and Reese goes to grab her jacket.

"Excuse me?" I give her a weird look.

"What?" She looks confused.

"It's your turn."

"Oh." She looks surprised. *Do girls not usually want to take care of her?* She is flipping gorgeous with this banging body. I am dying for a taste, honestly.

"Come here." I give her my best come hither look, and she bites her bottom lip. Yes, this is about to be amazing. I am sure of it.

We're back to kissing, this time she's against the wall and I'm taking the lead. The way I like it, she is going to be soaked under my touch. I pull up her black t-shirt and her Calvin Klein sports bra to reveal two perky breasts. I audibly moan and I swear she blushes, but my head is between her breasts before I know for sure. I place open mouth kisses all over her chest, nibbling on her nipples and leaving behind hickies on her breasts. It is my signature move.

She groans as I pop her nipple out of my mouth, swirling it around with my tongue. Then I reach for her belt, untangling it and unbuttoning her jeans. I take my rings off my right hand and swap them to my left. No one wants to be fingered with jewelry, that shit hurts worse than long nails. Thankfully I had my manicurist cut a few of my fingers just a bit shorter than the rest. I regularly hook up with women and I din't want anyone wondering if I am straight.

I tug down her black thong and squeeze her ass. I'm about to go down on her when I realize I'll have to kneel on the ground. Sure this bathroom is clean, but it is still a *bathroom*. I walk away from Reese and her eyes flutter open, her jaw dropping.

"Uh?" She looks at me confused when I reach for

toilet paper. I fold up two squares and place them on the ground before her, placing one knee on each.

"Oh my gosh, you good now, princess?" Reese chuckles.

"Hey, I don't want to get all dirty."

"I thought you liked it dirty." Reese winks.

Instead of replying, I dive into her pussy with my tongue. Sucking lightly on her core, I lick up and down her slit, taking all of her in. I was right, she tastes amazing. Somehow sweeter than I expected and I want to lap up every drop of it.

"Oh fuck, baby," Reese moans under my touch. Her hand reaches for my hair, gripping the back of my head and holding it steady.

I continue listening to her moans and whimpers as I go faster and faster with my tongue. I flatten my tongue against her core, and that causes her to cry out my name. Something that has never sounded hotter than in this moment. I can feel myself getting wet again, something about giving a woman pleasure really gets me going. I slide in a finger in her tight core and she almost falls into me. Reese is soaked, her pussy giving away just how much she is attracted to me. It is hot as hell, my face is drenched in her and I am loving every second of it.

"Oh! Right there. Please don't stop." Reese bucks her hips, and I keep my pace. My jaw is working overtime to keep going while my hand is starting to cramp, but I don't let up. When a woman tells you not to stop, you keep fucking going and deal with the consequences later.

"Oh! Fuck, fuck, fuck!" Reese screams out, and I smile against her as her legs begin to shake. She utters a whole bunch of curses as she rides out her orgasm, only stopping when she finally pushes my head away.

She lifts her panties and jeans, then helps me stand up. I pick up the toilet paper I was using for my knees and throw it in the toilet, flushing it down. Reese grabs her motorcycle jacket while I wash my hands at the sink. We're both quiet as Reese regains her breath and I fix my hair in the mirror, it is thankfully only slightly out of place.

"So..." Reese gives me a look, but I walk over and kiss her. I am always a sucker for kissing after sex, not just for another taste but because I love kissing. Something about it being foreplay is as much aftercare for me. Probably something to do with intimacy, but I push that thought away. That will be a question for my therapist.

"That was fun." I smile, pulling away from her soft lips.

"It was," Reese agrees.

This is that awkward moment where I'll have to say it wouldn't happen again. I don't do relationships, not right now anyway. It isn't fair to start anything when I am so helplessly into Bella. *Fuck*, I try so hard not to think about her. Especially after sex. But here I am torturing myself with the thought of my best friend that I know I can never be with.

"So, I guess I'll see you around?" Reese says, but I can't tell if it is a statement or a question.

"Probably not." I shrug. It was fun, Reese is definitely the hottest lay I've had in a while, but I know it isn't going to be anything more than that. No point in getting anyone's hopes up.

"Okay, cool then." Reese looks relieved. *Does every*

girl she hooked up with suddenly fall in love with her or something? I know she has a good tongue and a nice pussy but that isn't anything to fall in love over.

"Well, bye then," I say with a nervous laugh and head out the bathroom door. I find my way back to my friends.

"Where have you been?" Bella asks anxiously.

"Fucking a hot girl," I say, hoping it will elicit some kind of a reaction from her. It never does and each time I'm disappointed. I don't know why I play this game with myself.

"The girl from before?" Morgan asks.

"Yup," I say proudly. There was once a time where Morgan and I tied for number of one night stands and girls we could pick up at bars. Sometimes I wish she was still that person, but I know she's happier now with her insta family.

"Her friend is cool, Mitchell. We danced with him for a bit but he ditched us for some guy," Morgan explains.

"Are you ready to go to the other bar?" Bella asks.

"Are we done here?" I ask confused. *We haven't been at Puzzles that long, have we?* I am lost on all track of time thanks to my activities in the bathroom. I pick up my phone from my back pocket and look at the time, we've only been here a little over an hour.

"Well, Dylan said she's on her way to the second place on our list. I thought it would be nice to get there first so she doesn't have to wait outside." Bella bites her bottom lip, explaining. *Why do I have to find it so cute when she does that? Or when she does anything, for that matter.*

"Ah." I bite my jaw and force a smile. "Well, we don't want to keep her waiting."

Morgan shoots me a look but I don't say anything. It probably came out sassier than I intended, but I don't care. I just follow as my friends leave their empty drink glasses behind and lead the way out the door. It's chillier than it was before, the crisp March air hitting us the second we leave. I'm not as drunk as I should be to ignore it. I should've done some shots or something before we left. Knowing that I am going to meet my best friends possible new girlfriend, I am going to need at least ten. We ride the crowded subway to the next place, and I let Morgan and Bella handle the conversation this time. I'm too lost in my thoughts about Bella to care enough to converse.

It is bad enough being in love with someone you can't have, your best friend no less. But to watch your best friend be with someone else? I don't think that is something I am ready to do. Yet here we are, only two stops away from my own personal hell.

Chapter 4

Reese

"Where the hell have you been?" Mitchell finds me on my second loop around the bar, looking for him.

"Uh, looking for you." I hold out his phone. It was kind of stupid of me to take it from him on such a busy holiday. I didn't think I'd find him this quickly.

"I saw you leave with the pink haired woman, what happened?" He rolls his eyes.

"You know I don't like to kiss and tell." I wink. But to be honest, it is the first time I've had a one night stand with someone I wouldn't mind seeing again. She'd been so nonchalant when she left, is that how it feels to be left by me?

"Oh please, she was so into you."

"Weren't you with her friends?" I had waited a few minutes before leaving the bathroom, grabbing a shot of vodka on the way out. Is she still here somewhere? Not that I care.

"I was, but then there was this hot guy. So I was

dancing with him for a bit but apparently he was trying to make his boyfriend jealous and then there was almost a fight." He throws his hands in the air in defense. "It was too much testosterone for me."

"You love testosterone," I point out.

"Not that kind. Too much of men trying to fight each other so I dipped." He shrugs.

"Are you ready to get out of here then?"

"You're not meeting up with your new friend?" Mitchell teases.

"Come on, you know I do one night stands. She's just a stranger I ate out in the bar bathroom." I shrug it off like it's no big deal. Even though part of me is still thinking about her. What the heck is up with that anyway?

"Oh gross." He pretends like he's going to barf. We can help each other pick up people, but talk about sex and suddenly we remember our relationship is like brother and sister. We're too platonic to think about the other even having sex, of course he's more dramatic about it than I am.

"Let's hit the party at McClaren's, they're doing cheap shots all night," I remind him.

"I could use one, or five." He laughs.

"So could I." I nod.

We grab an Uber outside Puzzles and drive the ten blocks downtown to McClaren's. We probably could've taken the subway but I am too lazy and Mitchell hates public transportation. We pull up right out front and since Mitchell and I know the bouncer, we're let in right away. Sometimes it pays to know a little bit of everyone in New York City.

This bar is smaller than Puzzles, but it has three floors. Each floor with a full bar and tables to grab some food at. Mitchell and I head upstairs to the second floor to grab a booth in the back by the windows. It has a view overlooking the streets nearby so maybe we can catch a glimpse of the parade. Mitchell is more into the parade than I am, I'm not a fan of the music and bagpipes they have playing throughout it. They are one of the worst instruments invented in my opinion.

Thankfully the back table is empty except for a few dirty cups that a waitress happily removes for us. We order shots of vodka, an order of buffalo wings, and some beer. Mitchell watches the parade while I glance around the bar. There are mostly groups of guys watching sports on the televisions, a few of them cheering as they drink beer and eat onion rings. I know it is more of a sports bar, so I won't have too many prospects here. Not that women can't go to sports bars, especially women into women, but it is rare to find some already not taken.

"Do you want to play pool?" Mitchell glances at the pool table and I nod. He knows I am a shark at pool and I won't turn down a game.

"Hell yeah!" I throw down the shot of vodka in front of me and wipe the buffalo wing residue off my hands. I want to be on top of my game here, not letting greasy hands hold me back.

We make our way to the other side of the room, where the pool table is. I start setting up the balls while Mitchell gets the pool sticks. He carefully picks his out and then hands me a random one, as if that'll give me some disadvantage. I've yet to lose a game of pool against him in all our years of friendship. I finish setting up and Mitchell insists on going first. Letting him, he lines himself up and manages to miss getting any balls in.

"Better luck next time?" I laugh and get ready for my turn. I line myself up, ready to go when I catch a glimpse of pink in my peripheral vision. I stop, is that Ellie and her pink hair? My hand slips and I hit the ball, but none of them go in the hole, but my eyes are on the door. Ellie and her friends are walking in, looking for a booth to sit in, headed right for mine and Mitchell's.

"What?! Did Reese just miss a shot? An *easy* shot?" Mitchell is teasing me but I can barely hear him. My eyes are on Ellie and her curves. *What did this woman do to me?*

I walk away from him, putting my stick down and reaching our table at the same moment Ellie does. "What, are you following me?" I say sassily.

"Shit, Reese?" Ellie's eyes widen at the sight of me.

"What are you doing here?" I ask.

"We were hoping to grab some food, we're meeting some people. But there seems to be no tables left in the place," Ellie explains.

"This is our booth but you can join us, right Mitch?" I call and he nods, walking over.

"Hello again, ladies." He smiles.

"Dylan is here, let me go grab her," the brunette says, I think her name starts with a B but I can't tell you what it was. She leaves the group as I move our drinks out of the way for them to sit. I watch Ellie's face change as she watches her friend leave the place. *What is going on there?*

"I'm Morgan by the way, we kind of met before."

The other brunette holds out her hand and smiles. I shake it and nod.

"Reese."

"We were just playing some pool if you want to join us," Mitchell adds. "Someone was just losing."

"Excuse me, one bad shot does not make one a loser," I remind him.

"Pool? Ellie is AH-mazing at pool." Morgan smiles.

"You are?" I say, surprised.

"You don't have to seem so surprised." Ellie smirks.

"Can I get you guys anything?" the waitress interrupts.

"I'd love a shot of whiskey and some fries." Ellie smiles.

"Great, and you?" The waitress looks at Morgan.

"Those wings look good and maybe a vodka cranberry? Two actually," Morgan adds.

"Why don't you show me how good you think you are?" I direct the conversation back to pool.

"Only if you're prepared to lose." Ellie smirks.

"Challenge accepted." I wink. "After you." She leads the way, but it's just an excuse for me to stare at her ass. Each step a perfect jiggle and shake.

"Are you staring at my ass?" Ellie turns around, and I don't change where I'm looking.

"Fuck yeah, I am." I laugh. "It's a nice ass."

Ellie laughs, and I swear a blush creeps over her cheeks. But she doesn't tell me to stop so I appreciate the view. She takes over Mitchell's spot as he joins Morgan at the table so he can finish his wings. I think it is his way of pushing Ellie and I together even though that is pointless. I mean she is cool but it isn't like this is going to turn into something.

"Now don't get any ideas here, this is just two strangers playing pool," Ellie says as if she's reading my mind.

"Hey, you're the one who's following me. Should I be concerned and take out a restraining order?" I tease.

"Maybe, you know I just can't get enough of your pussy." She leans in, close enough for me to smell her soft lilac perfume, whispering the last word. Then she aligns herself with the cue ball and makes a shot, hitting two balls in the pockets at once.

"Damn," I say, suddenly impressed.

"Told you I was good." She winks and shakes her hips. Maybe I could break my one night stand rule for just another time, I mean it is still the same day after all. And after the way she ate me out earlier, I definitely was impressed. Not many women can make me cum like that, or at all.

"My turn." I grab my stick and pay close attention this time. I want her to know I'm not just all talk. Thankfully I hit it and a ball lands in the far left pocket. Not as good as I wanted, but it will do.

"Nice, almost as much as me," she teases then stiffens. I glance at her eye line and see that she's staring at her friend with a B, and the girlfriend she just went to get, Dylan? I think that is her name. I really need to work on paying attention. Ellie stiffens at the sight of them and that's when it hits me. Is Ellie secretly into her friend? Or maybe not so secretly? Something is clearly going on there if the sight of them holding hands is enough to set her off.

"Your turn," I prompt her.

"Oh." She doesn't have a smart comeback this time or anything sassy to say to me. She takes her turn and doesn't even gloat when she makes another ball in.

"You good?" I ask after a few minutes of her silence.

She looks up at me with a puzzled look on her face, glances at the table of her friends, and then back to me. But instead of saying anything, she pulls me in for a kiss. Her body presses against mine and my back into the pool table as her tongue slips into my mouth. I'm surprised, but I go for it at the same time. My hands use her waist to steady myself as we continue kissing. I can't tell if she's doing it to make the girl jealous or because she wants me, but I'm not complaining. It isn't the first time I've been used.

"Do you wanna get out of here?" she asks, copying my words from earlier. No, she can't be sleeping with me to make someone jealous, right?

"Yes." I nod, murmuring against her lips.

I take her by the hand and lead her past the table, where I watch her not look at her friends, and downstairs to the first floor. I was going to take her to the bathroom again but this time there's a huge line of women waiting to go in. I don't want to wait on any kind of line and then have people knocking and hurrying us along. So I keep her hand in mine and lead her down the hallway to a closet. I hope she won't ask me how I know it is here because I don't have a classy answer for her.

We step inside, closing the door behind us, and I pull on the light switch, you know the kind the long string in the middle of the room. It illuminates just enough for us to see the bottles of chemicals and rat poison. Not exactly your aphrodisiacs, but it will have to do for now.

"Are you sure you want to do this?" I ask, double checking. As much as I am turned on for her, I don't want to fuck someone for the wrong reasons. She gives me a weird look but hesitates.

"Yes, it doesn't have to mean anything though, right?" *Oh, that's what she is worried about.* Here I am reading into things and she's probably worried I'm gaining feelings for her.

"It's nothing more than a good time, babe, trust me," I reassure her.

"Perfect." She leans into me, our bodies pressing against one another as our lips find each others.

She wastes no time taking off her t-shirt this time and tossing it to the side. I do the same, thankful I left my jacket behind this time. It is my favorite and I don't go anywhere without it, I don't want it to accidentally get bleached or some shit. I stand before her in my sports bra as she looks me over like a piece of meat. Oh yeah, there is no doubting this woman is attracted to me. She ties back her long, pink, curls with a hair tie and begins kissing my neck. She sucks lightly, not hard enough to leave any evidence, and I moan in her ear.

"Fuck," I whisper as she takes my breasts one at a time in her mouth. I am hoping she'll eat me out again. Last time she was too damn cute putting down paper before she got down on her knees. Seeing her all pink hair and closed eyes while she devoured my pussy was something else.

"I want you," she whispers back, and I make it my mission to make her cum for me.

I tug down her jeans in one swift movement, her panties falling close behind and she does the same for me. I palm her already wet core and trail my fingers through her slit. I brush softly against her clit, enjoying how she bucks her body into my hand at the slightest touch. But karma happens quickly when she does the same to me. Copying my hand motions on my core. I look into her eyes as I slide in one finger, keeping my thumb pressed against her clit, and her breath hitches.

"Oh, Reese," she moans against me, and I wink. I'm about to start moving my fingers when she inserts one finger and presses her thumb against my clit. I'm weak in the knees from the teasing she's doing, but I can tell she's enjoying it. We are two alphas playing with fire, fighting for dominance when we both want to succumb to the pleasure.

"Fuck me," I mumble, and within the second her lips are crashing into mine. Neither of us wanting to give in.

Ellie inserts another finger so I do the same, but this time I don't pause to see what she'll do. I keep going, pumping quick and hard, feeling all her wetness dripping on my hand. She does the same, fingering me with a steady feeling on my clit. We were both riding each other's hands, kissing and dying for a release that the other can provide. Silent moans and gasps are all to be heard as we fuck as quietly as we can. Ellie's the first to cum, a flick of my fingers on her g-spot is the way to do it, and she cums beautifully under my touch. Some people look weird when they cum, but fuck, not Ellie. Her mouth forms a perfect little o, with her pink lips and her hair flying behind her, she looks like something in a movie. Maybe a dirty movie, but a movie I'd watch on repeat.

"Oh fuck." Her hand stops moving just for a moment but the second she rides through her orgasm she's fingering me again, her hand working harder this time. I can feel myself getting closer and closer, but it's as she uses her free hand to wrap it around her throat that I finish. She smirks as I keep my eyes open to watch her. She is so fucking hot, I want to see the woman who gives me the mind blowing orgasm.

Chapter 5

Ellie

Reese pulls up her pants, and I do the same. Something I didn't think I'd get to do twice in one day, but then again, I don't have the best coping skills. Seeing Bella with Dylan is harder than I expected and I know it isn't right, but Reese is here and I just need to not feel my feelings for Bella for a little while. But now we are on our way back upstairs and I can tell it's going to feel just as shitty for me. It's not like I used Reese, okay maybe a little bit. But I do like her, like she is hot and sexy and an amazing kisser. So what is the harm if we both want a little release with no strings attached? It's not like either of us are looking for anything more than that. If we were I never would've kissed her again. Of course, part of me, a little part, had hoped it would make Bella jealous. But once I saw that wasn't working, I just wanted something to numb my feelings besides alcohol.

"Look who's back," Morgan teases when we make our way back to the table. I sit next to Bella so I don't have to see her and Dylan's faces. I know it's lame of me but I have big feelings and I'm a little too drunk to be mature today.

"Yes, yes. Sorry you missed us," Reese teases, not skipping a beat. She winks and takes a seat across from me and next to Mitchell.

"So, I texted that guy," he announces as if we're all supposed to know what he's talking about.

"What guy?" Morgan asks at the same time Reese angrily says, "No, you didn't."

"Hey, you were gone. I was lonely," he defends himself. He ignores his best friend's scowl and turns to Morgan. "This guy who's number I got at the bar today. He's super cute."

"But I told him to wait to text." Reese rolls her eyes.

"Eh, I met my girlfriend after a one night stand where I was interviewing to be her nanny. Romance doesn't always have a formula," Morgan says with a shrug and sips her drink.

I wait for Reese to say something sassy back, but she doesn't. Bella and Dylan are whispering things to each other next to me, and I have to fight the urge to listen in. I don't want to know what they're talking about, especially if it has anything to do with them sneaking off together.

"Excuse me," Bella says to me. She wants to be let out of the booth, and I wonder if it's to go hookup somewhere.

I stand to let her out of the booth and Dylan follows close behind. It's the second or third time we've met so I'm grateful we didn't have to shake hands or anything. I give her a polite smile before sitting back down. But in the corner of my eye, I see Bella and Dylan starting to play pool. Except unlike me, Bella's never played pool a day in her life. So Dylan, of course, is holding the stick behind her and guiding it like we're in some kind of fucking rom-com. It is disgusting. My face must be saying everything I'm thinking because suddenly I'm being kicked under the table.

"Ow." I rub my shin and look up at Morgan. She has a habit of doing that when I am being too obvious about my feelings.

"Whoops, sorry, leg slipped." She lies perfectly so no one suspects anything. Reese gives us a weird look but stands to grab herself another drink from the bar.

Mitchell's busy texting the guy he shouldn't be, so Morgan leans closer to me and whispers, "You're being too obvious." I know she means well, but fuck, she doesn't know what it is like. It was bad enough when Bella was single and I had to worry about all the people she could be meeting as a fucking escort, but now? It is like I have no chance in hell of ever being with her. Not that I ever would've told her about my feelings, but I liked having the option to. Now, with Dylan, the option is gone. Sure, one could argue that I could still tell her how I feel but I am not the type to want to get in the middle of someone's relationship. Bella is happy, can't that be enough?

I glance at my friend, but she's currently in the middle of a lip-lock and my heart breaks. I pound down the drink in front of me and immediately, I stand and rush out of there. I don't even know where I'm going but I know I can't be there anymore. I go down the few flights of stairs and outside the bar. I'm standing outside for a few minutes alone, trying to catch my breath in the freezing cool air, when a hand touches my shoulder.

"Here, you look like you need this." Reese hands me

her jacket and without thinking, I put it on. What surprises me most is how it fits. We aren't exactly the same size, my curves not being a secret, but it must be big on Reese because it fits just enough to keep my arms warm.

"Thanks," I mumble. I can't help but notice how warm it feels like she'd been wearing it and how good it smells. Reese tends to smell like beer and cinnamon, but this jacket just smells like cinnamon and some kind of body spray. It is almost manly but with a feminine touch as if she added perfume to her body spray. I like it.

"Do you want to talk about it?" Reese asks after a moment.

"Talk about what?" I ask, playing dumb.

"The fact that you're into your friend, the one with the B name."

"Bella?" I ask even though I know the answer. She nods but I stay silent.

"Why would you think I'm into her?"

"It's quite obvious," Reese says shrugging. "It's okay, I don't mind being used." She cracks a smile so I know that she's teasing me. *Am I really that obvious if complete strangers are picking up on it? Does that mean Bella knows too?*

"I don't know what you're talking about. I'm not into my best friend, I mean how could I be?" I say defensively.

"Okay, you're totally not." Reese chuckles.

"I'm sorry," I start apologizing. "I'm really sorry, I shouldn't have-"

"Please don't finish that sentence because I think we both know that what we did wasn't you using me or making anyone jealous. You did that because you wanted to." Reese gives me a look and I nod. She was right, I did want to.

"It'll be okay," she says.

"How would you know? Did you have a best friend you were into?"

"Well, actually I did," Reese admits.

"And how's that working out for you?" I point out. It can't be going well considering our meeting circumstances.

"Touché." She chuckles.

"I don't want to like her," I point out.

"I get that, you can't help who you fall for. But it must suck having to see her be with someone else." She sighs and leans against the wall with me.

"It really does." I nod, ignoring the tears brimming in my eyes. I am willing them away, the last thing I want to do right now is cry to my one night stand about the girl I am in love with. Not that I think Reese will care, but I just can't. I wipe them away subtly and think about anything else but this moment.

"The girl I liked was my friend too. She knew I went through a rough time and told me I was 'confused'. Not about liking girls or anything, but just confused about liking her. She stopped talking to me three days later," Reese says with a shrug.

"Women suck." I shake my head.

"People suck," she corrects me and I laugh.

"Amen to that."

"So tell me, what do you do?" Reese changes the subject.

"I'm... well, I'm someone who brings coffee to someone who is a fashion designer. I'm at an internship right now." I sigh. This isn't making me feel much better either, I am hating my job these days.

"Is your goal to become a fashion designer?" Reese guesses.

"Yes. I'd like to have my own store on Fifth Avenue with the high end mannequins," I admit.

"So what's stopping you?"

"Time. I have to pay my dues before I can really make it, so right now that's all I can do." I pause. "But I do design on the side, to keep up with my craft but also in case I was ever asked to make anything."

"That's impressive. Do you think you can get away without paying your dues with a job you hate?"

"Am I really that obvious?" I laugh.

"Only a little," Reese teases.

"I mean maybe, but it might be a lot harder on me and take me twice as long." I hadn't really considered building my name up any other way.

"Isn't your happiness worth that?"she points out. I pause. Of course it is, that is a no brainer. But giving up my job that would open doors upon doors just to start at the bottom seemed crazy.

"Of course, but it's more complicated than that. I mean, what do you do?"

"I'm a barista, who's still trying to figure out her purpose in life," Reese says confidently. Normally I'd think anyone who's working at a coffee shop has a dead end job, but Reese says it with such confidence you can't help but believe she'll do whatever she sets her mind to.

"So you make coffee to pay the bills?"

"They must get paid somehow." She chuckles.

"What gives you joy?" I ask.

"Definitely not my job." She laughs.

"See, so it's not uncommon for people to hate their job. I can't just quit mine because I hate it."

"I'm not saying you should quit, but I also leave my hatred for the job at work. Do you take it home with you? It's written all over your face when you talk about it."

"I just...my boss is kind of like the woman from *The Devil Wears Prada*. She's ruthless and sometimes I think she's testing me to see if I'll break and quit." I sigh. I hate Veronica but I know it is only a few more months of working under her and hopefully I'll be on the right track to getting out of there.

"So you want to prove her wrong and that you can keep up with all she throws at you?" Reese guesses.

"Yes. Because I can," I say confidently.

"I see." She nods.

Reese has somehow made me forget why I even came outside in the first place. It is like the thought of Bella and Dylan is becoming less intense. I don't know if it was the alcohol I had, or Reese making it better. She's distracted me with a real conversation, she hangs on to every word I say. She isn't bored about what I have to say, she hasn't belittled my feelings, she just lets things be. I appreciate that, sometimes it is nice just to have someone to listen.

She's looking at the crowd of people huddled by the front door, waiting to get in. I study her face for a moment, it's one of the first times I'm seeing her up close that we aren't otherwise preoccupied. She's beautiful, there's no denying that. Her jaw is sharp, her thick, black hair is short and lays cropped on her head, but she has these beautiful thick eyelashes to match.

Her eyes are dark, closer to black than brown and she doesn't wear any makeup so this is all natural beauty. I look away before she can catch me staring, but I appreciate the silence to catch my thoughts. Some people are afraid of silences but I like them. They don't make me nervous or anxious, they give me a minute to think about what I want to say next. It is clear Reese is comfortable with them too.

"Do you want to head back inside?" I ask Reese.

"Only when you do." She smiles. It's a small gesture but it means more than I'll let on.

"Is it bad that I'm contemplating leaving them here?" I joke.

"Yes, but also no. You shouldn't have to sit through and watch that gross pda."

"It was gross right!? Something about it was just icky."

"It's called being jealous," Reese says with a pretend cough.

"I'm not jealous, I just...maybe wish they weren't together." I look at Reese and we both laugh. It is easy talking to her, somehow she just gets how I am feeling. Maybe because she has experienced it too.

"The green eyed monster can be a deadly thing."

"I know, I know. I'm trying so hard to preserve the friendship but it's killing me a bit more lately," I admit.

"It's not the letting go that hurts, it's the holding on."

"You sound like a fortune cookie, you know." I laugh.

"I've been told I'm wise, but never that I sound like a cookie." She cracks a smile.

If this were a rom-com, I think this would be the

moment that we'd kiss. Reese and I would see fireworks for the first time and we'd both feel inclined to see each other again. But of course this isn't a rom-com, the best I will do is ask for her number but just as I'm thinking about how to word it, the door swings open between us.

"Um, I think he belongs to you." Morgan is holding Mitchell up with one arm.

"Mitch?" Reese looks at him concerned.

"He was doing shots and we think he drank a little too much. He wanted to come out here alone, but I didn't think that was a good idea," Morgan explains. God bless the mother in her. Mitchell is clearly intoxicated and those stairs are no joke when you are sober.

"I got him, thank you." Reese takes him under her arm.

"Reese! When did you get here?" He smiles happily.

"Oh yeah, we're going to head home, buddy." Reese chuckles. She starts walking away but pauses to turn around and look at me.

"It was nice talking to you," I say awkwardly. I mean what do you say to someone you hooked up with twice but then admitted you had feelings for someone else to?

"It was. I'll see you around, Ellie." She winks and I blush.

"Oh wait! Your jacket." I start to shrug it off but she stops me.

"Keep it, it looks better on you anyway." Reese smiles and takes off down the street to call a cab.

Chapter 6

Ellie

1 year later...

"Are you sure about this?" I look at my therapist, unconvinced.

"The real question is, are you ready for this?" She moves the glasses up the bridge of her nose, and I sigh. I hate when she asks me questions like that, I mean who knows for sure if they are ever ready for something?

"I think so."

"Walk me through your thoughts," she instructs.

"I haven't been on a date in months—scratch that, almost a year. I feel like I'm finally over Bella and I can handle being in a relationship again," I admit. It had been a long and hard road getting over my best friend but with therapy and a lot of time and space, I finally feel like I've moved on. Bella's still with Dylan and I no longer feel like I want to rip their heads off every time they have pda when I'm around. Instead I actually feel happy for them, and maybe a little jealous I haven't found that for myself yet.

"Then what's stopping you?" she asks, pointing her chin at me.

"I don't know, I guess nothing." I shrug. It is a breaking point for me, I mean why can't I start dating again? I have been a one night stand junkie for some time now because of my feelings but with them being gone, I am able to commit to someone new.

"Do you feel like you want this?"

"Yes. I've wanted to move on for awhile, but especially now that I'm over Bella, I want to get back out there and see if I can find what my friends have with their partner,." I explain.

"Then I think your task for the week is to join a dating app, make a profile, and just ease into it." She closes the notebook on her lap to let me know the session is over.

On my way home, I scroll through my phone contemplating downloading an app. Tomorrow is St. Patrick's Day and for the first time in years I don't have any plans. Morgan is spending the day taking Lucy and Noel to the parade while Dylan and Bella are having a quiet day at their apartment. It bums me out a bit that it is the end of an era of going out, but I know we are getting older. Maybe having a date for the holiday won't make me feel so alone. Can I find a date that quickly? I know I could if it was in person, I have no problem meeting women, but I have never tried my luck on an app.

Sighing, I download tinder to my phone and start to create a profile. The bio is easy, I put my birth sign; Gemini, my career; fashion designer, and what I'm looking for; something casual or something real. It feels nice to be able to actually say I'm a designer now. It was a rough few months as an intern but I recently started preparing my own line under my old boss. Sure, she gets a lot of the credit, but it is my designs going out there. I am officially a designer and that can never be taken away from me.

I swipe aimlessly through the sea of women until I get a few matches. I'm into more masculine women, so it takes some time to weed through the more feminine women. I'm not into waiting so I message them all first, looking at their bio to say something about them and see if they'll reply. I am better at communicating in person, this whole online thing is a mystery to me, I feel like an old person. My phone chimes with a message received and I realize it's a match replying to my message about liking her aesthetic. She has a ton of tattoos, short dark hair, and nice tan skin, she is beautiful on every level. I wait until I get off the train to reply, not wanting my shitty service to stand between me and the potential love of my life.

Ria: Thanks! I love your hair, super cute like you;)

Me: haha thank you. How's your day going?

Ria and I go back and forth for a bit while I get home and fold some laundry. I'm putting away the clean dishes and filling the dishwasher and she's asking me if I want to grab a drink sometime. *Is it really this easy to find someone to date?* I mean she seems nice enough so far. I ask her if she'd like to go out tomorrow and when she says she's free, I'm ecstatic. I won't be alone on St. Patricks Day and I'll have a good story to tell my therapist next week. She'll be proud of me just for downloading the stupid app and here I am excelling already.

What am I going to wear? It is St. Patrick's Day,

after all, so I have to wear something green but it is also a first date. I don't know how many first date worthy outfits I had that are green. I sigh and stumble toward my oversized closet, pawing through my clothes. I think about what I wore last year and my eyes jump to the back of my door where Reese's jacket hangs.

For the better part of a year, it had hung on the back of my door as a silent reminder of that day. Reese and I never saw each other after that, no matter how often I thought we might. But that is probably for the best, sometimes it is good to leave things the way they are. I walk over and take down the jacket, holding it close and sniffing it lightly. It still smells like her. Don't ask me how I can remember a smell from someone a year ago, sometimes things like that just stick with you.

I throw it on the bed, and head back to my closet, searching for a green top to wear. I find a jean mini skirt and a green long sleeve v-neck. It will look perfect with the jacket and it's not like I can't wear it, she had said it looked good on me anyway. Putting it next to my bed, I leave it for the morning and text Ria goodnight before heading to sleep, excited for the next day.

☘ ☘ ☘

IN THE MORNING I get dressed in a hurry, doing my makeup and hair more quickly than necessary. I don't want to keep Ria waiting, we had said we'd meet at Puzzles at twelve and I know traffic is going to be insane. I don't want to give a bad first impression by being late. I take the subway, walking isn't an option in these boots. They are cute as hell but definitely not for walking, not to mention it snowed overnight, making me have to stick tights under my skirt. I'm not going to attempt walking through the snow in any outfit, but especially this one.

I had Sawyer put me on the list at Puzzles again just in case I decided to go out on my own, and I'm relieved I did. I text Ria to say my name at the door and head inside to get out of the cold. I head over to the bar where Cody is bartending again this year.

"Look who it is!" he teases with a smile on his face.

"Hi, don't make such a fuss, people are staring," I joke, like staring would ever bother me. I am used to looks from being plus size and having cotton candy hair. It is something I embrace, not shy away from.

"Oh please, where's your posse?" He looks behind me confused, knowing I'm not usually alone.

"They ditched me today, but it's okay because I have a hot date," I say proudly.

"Nice, can I get you a drink while you wait?" I probably shouldn't because I am already nervous and my knee is bouncing a million miles a minute, but I nod. He pours something green in front of me and I down it before asking what it was.

"Wow, that nervous, huh?" Cody's eyes widen.

"Yes," I admit. If you can't be honest with your bartender, who can you be honest with?

"What time is she due?" He glances at the clock and I stiffen in my seat.

"Now."

"Oh boy, good luck." He chuckles and heads over to help someone across the bar.

There's an empty seat next to me that I keep open

by putting my hand on. I try not to check my phone but after ten minutes, I want to see if she's running late or something. We never exchanged numbers, keeping everything in the app so I open Tinder to see if there's a message. To my surprise, Ria's profile is gone and so are our messages. *What the hell?* Where did she go? Did I accidentally delete her or something? I know I was new to this but surely I wasn't so technologically disadvantaged that I deleted her, right?

"Hey! Cody!" I call him over. He holds up a finger and comes by a few minutes later.

"What's up?"

"Can you tell me if I'm stupid. This girl was here and now she's gone. Is there a way to get her back?"

"Uh." Cody's face pales and I raise an eyebrow.

"What?"

"I think she ghosted you," he says quietly. My eyes widen. I don't live under a rock, I know about ghosting, but I've never had it happen to me.

"Are you sure?" I ask.

"Well, if you didn't delete her then yes." He gives me one of those awkward smiles and heads back to work.

What the actual fuck? Why would someone just ghost like that? It's not like I did anything. Even if I had, telling me would be a hell of a lot better than just vanishing from thin air. I hadn't heard from her since last night, but I thought we were still on for today. Jeez, I feel like such a loser. I apparently have a lot to learn about online dating. Now I am going to have to spend my St. Patrick's Day alone. Cody brings over a green drink on the house and I begin to drown my sorrows in my drink. It is bad enough all my friends have ditched me, but now I was ditched by someone who didn't even get the chance to know me? That shit just sucks.

I'm about to go home and drown my sadness in cheese doodles and ice cream when a familiar voice startles me out of my thoughts. "I said you looked better in my jacket."

Chapter 7

Reese

I spot her from across the bar, just like I did a year earlier. Like something out of a rom-com, this woman and I are destined to keep finding each other in bars. Well, at least this one. But it's when I see her wearing my jacket that I can't help but smile. She kept it all this time *and* she is wearing it? I wonder if that means she's thought about me as much as I've thought about her.

I have always been a womanizer, a one night stand savant, but since meeting Ellie, I couldn't get her out of my head. It's not like I was suddenly a relationship gal, I have my fair share of trauma. But there was something about her that made me wonder if I'd ever see her again. If I'd ever run into her at a bar, or on the subway. Despite how big New York City is, it happens more often than you think. So I'm equally surprised and unsurprised by the fact that we are running into each other today of all days.

"I said you looked better in my jacket." I smirk and she turns around with a huge smile on her face.

"Reese?" She looks at me surprised. Her pink hair is even longer, her makeup almost identical to last year's, but she's wearing an even sexier outfit this year. A skirt to show off her thick thighs and her fuck me boots that I'd love to see over my shoulders.

"Hey, El." I make her name even shorter, still not knowing if Ellie is short for anything.

"What are you doing here?" She pats the stool next to her and I happily take a seat.

"It's St. Patrick's Day, I always come to Puzzles." I laugh. "What are you doing here?"

"Well." She pauses. "I was supposed to be on a date."

"Oh." I try to hide my reaction. Of course she is seeing someone, I mean it has been a year after all.

"No, but they, uh, ghosted me," she says shyly. Her shoulders slump, her body sighing with disappointment.

"Their loss is my gain." I wink with a smirk. Her shoulders perk back up and a smile crosses her face. "Where are your friends this year?"

"They all had plans with their significant others." There's no bitterness when she says this, as if it's just her friends being in relationships. I wonder if that means she was over her friend. I mean, it has been a year after all.

"I see," I say nonchalantly, like I don't care that much. Even though I kind of do. What is it about this woman to bring out this side of me?

"I see you're wearing green this year." She nods toward my green t-shirt.

"Hey, someone pinched me last year and I'm still bruised from it," I joke.

Lucky to be Yours

"Oh, I didn't pinch you that hard!" She laughs. Light and airy, just like I remember. Like music to my ears.

"It was memorable. Like you," I add. I know it's cheesy but I can't seem to help myself.

"Someone's looking to have a repeat quickie in the bathroom," she teases. I hope that's not what she is really thinking. I mean sure, I'll take her back there in an instant, but this feels different.

"Nah, I think I'm actually looking to take a pretty Irish gal to dinner this year," I admit, surprising myself.

"Shit, am I not in the running then?" Ellie pretends to be disappointed.

"What?" I ask confused.

"I'm not Irish." She laughs, and I face palm myself.

"Well, a fake Irish gal then. Someone who wears a lot of green," I add for good measure.

"Damn, there's a lot of those here today. I have some stiff competition," she mocks.

"Oh shush, will you let me take you out?"

"Only if we go anywhere but a bar." Ellie laughs.

"Yes, we can go anywhere." I nod.

"I know the perfect spot." Ellie smiles mischievously, and I wonder where she plans on taking me, but I don't ask. I like a little element of surprise every now and then.

Ellie closes out her tab at Puzzles, and I let her lead the way out of the bar. She grabs my hand to keep track of me in the crowd. I make it a point not to let go when we get outside and she doesn't either. I don't know if it's because of how nice it feels or because of how cold it is, but either way I'm not complaining.

"So, you were wearing my jacket to meet another

girl?" I ask, breaking the silence. I even raise an eyebrow to pretend that I'm upset about it.

"I mean you did say it was mine." She bites her bottom lip, looking at me worriedly.

"I'm just messing with you, I'm just glad it didn't work out for you." I wink.

"I forgot how much of a flirt you are." Ellie smiles, shaking her head.

"Only for you, babe." I wink again for good measure, and she blushes. It's a light pink that almost matches her hair.

"Come on." She drags me down the block and toward the subway.

"Subway?" I ask confused, how far was this place?

"Yes, why are you afraid of subways or something?" She pauses as if that is the only reason someone wouldn't want to ride the subway.

"No, I'm not afraid. I was just surprised it's that far." I shrug and follow her down the dirty steps to the train. We let go of each other's hands to swipe our metro cards through the turnstile and slide through.

I don't pick her hand up right away, looking around anxiously to see who is around first. There are only a few people and they seem harmless, mainly drunk college kids dressed in green. I hate that it is even something I have to worry about, but the last thing I want is me or Ellie getting harassed on the subway for holding hands. I have been through that too many times, knowing it is a hazard of riding the subway or being gay in public. My ex used to think I was overreacting, she'd take my hand anyway, but Ellie waits until I pick hers back up and smiles. I wonder if she thinks the way I do. If she's been a victim of the hatred of the world that I've seen too many times.

"You're a million miles away," Ellie says suddenly and stands a little closer to me.

"I was just thinking." I shrug.

"About what?"

"Nothing important," I lie. I don't want to open the door to worrying her if she doesn't have the same fears I do.

She studies my face for a moment but doesn't press it further and for that I'm thankful. The train stops in front of us, the wind whooshing in front of us, throwing her pink curls in disarray. I watch as she fixes it quickly with one hand, wrinkling her nose and hurrying us onto the train. There aren't any seats, just a pole in the middle of the train car for us to hold onto. I grab it with one hand and she grabs it with her free hand, our bodies facing each other's. The conductor murmurs something about the train running express and the doors close with a loud ding.

It's too quiet to have any kind of a conversation without the entire train hearing, so we both stay silent. Ellie smiles at me shyly and I look down at her lips. It's the first chance I've had to really study them this year. They are just as beautiful, looking just as soft and covered in red lipstick to really draw me toward them. She catches me looking but doesn't say anything, instead bites down on her bottom lip and I wiggle my eyebrows at her. Ellie blushes and I laugh quietly, thinking about how easy it is for me to get a reaction out of her.

The train stops short and I lose my footing, causing me to lose a few inches and crash into Ellie. She catches my arm, steadying me, and I stare deep into her light eyes. Pushing her hair out of her face, I take the opportunity to kiss her. It's something I've been thinking about for a year and there is no time like the present. Her lips part gently, inviting me to. It's a soft, slow, kiss but everything we both want in that moment. The train stops, opening the doors to more passengers, so we part to make way for them. I enjoy the smile and blush she leaves sitting on her face.

"The next stop is us," she says, clearing her throat after two more stops.

"Okay." I nod. I'm not familiar with this train or this stop so I have absolutely no idea where she is taking us. It is still just thrilling to be with her again.

Ellie takes my hand and leads us out of the train when the doors open again. We walk up more stairs than I care for and I'm almost out of breath by the time we reach the top. Why does the subway have to be in the literal depths of hell? The cold air hits us like a ton of bricks by the time we get outside. I had actually forgotten how freezing it is out today, my breath making smoke in front of me as we walk. Ellie is clearly on a mission to get us somewhere and she isn't making any pit stops. I am trailing behind, trying not to get lost in the chaos of the sea of green dressed people and the New Yorkers who are clearly pissed by the events of the day. But then again, when aren't New Yorkers always upset about something? It is in their blood to be pissed about it. I was born and raised in New Jersey so I have a little bit of the bitterness but not as much as say, Ellie who I can tell by her walk and the way she is ready to fight at any given second, she is a real New Yorker.

We walk through the fashion district, which I only

Lucky to be Yours

know from the signs I'm reading. Ellie still hasn't told me where we're headed and I'm not asking if I can help it. I can tell something is up from all the fabric stores and well dressed people. It is a nice break from the sea of green that I was getting used to. I start to wonder what we're doing here but then I remember what Ellie does for a living. Her favorite spot must be in the middle of the fashion district, I look down at my outfit. I'm dressed for anywhere too fancy but Ellie had to know that before we started this journey.

The buildings all look pretty similar until we get to one block. In the middle of all the tall cityscape, is an eyesore of a spot. It's a small two story building that has rotting red bricks and a bright green awning that is tearing in multiple spots. There's a sign on the actual building that I'm sure was lit up at one point but has long fizzled out. Shelly's! is what it reads, exclamation point and all. But what happens next is what surprises me the most.

"What do you think?" Ellie asks as we stop in front of the eyesore.

"What do you mean?" I think she's joking, but her face is serious as can be.

"This is my favorite spot in the city," she says with a huge smile on her face.

"This is seriously your *favorite* place?" I ask, unbelieving. The wooden door looks and sounds like it is going to fall off the hinges.

"It is." She laughs. "I know it doesn't look like much, and the coffee sucks. But these are the best bagels in the city."

"Well, now this is something I have to see to believe."

"Are you sure?"

"Yes, I asked for anywhere but a bar. You delivered. So show me why this place is your favorite." I step forward and open the creaky door, holding it open for her.

Inside is even more dated than the outside. It looks like this place hasn't had a makeover in over fifty years. The pale pink paint is peeling off the walls, there's an register at the front that's older than me, and I'm wondering if I have any cash on me because I doubt they take credit cards here. To my surprise, the place is crowded. Couples, families, and singles all filling up the booths and the seats at the counter. But like Ellie said, there isn't a single cup of coffee in sight. How bad is this coffee? I am half tempted to ask for a cup just to find out.

"Come on." Ellie takes my hand and brings me to a booth in the back. We both slide in the tearing leather seats and an older woman brings us over two menus. It must be some kind of a restaurant and cafe mix.

I try not to make a face as I look over the menu. The food all sounds good, muffins, cookies, bagels and sandwiches. But I'm a little hesitant to eat somewhere that looks so run down. It isn't like Ellie is some big savior of old restaurants, right? Or heck, maybe she is. I am still learning all there is to know about her. I glance at her over my menu and she's smiling away like a kid at Disneyland. So this is her favorite place, but why?

I look back at the menu, deciding on a bagel with cream cheese and bacon, just the way I like it. I normally would've paired it with a nice black coffee but instead I think some tea would go well. I'm sort of starving from not having eaten all day so I also opt for a blueberry muffin to satisfy my hunger.

"Do you know what you want?" Ellie smiles and I can't help but smile back.

"Yes." I explain my order and she nods.

"You order at the counter, I'll be right back."

"Crap, do you need money? I don't have any cash." I start feeling my pockets for my wallet.

"No, this is on me." She touches my shoulder as if to reassure me, and I do feel calmer.

Ellie heads to the front to wait on line and I look around the place. Trying to find a piece of what makes this place so special to Ellie. But it isn't easy. To me, this place looks like a dump. There are millions of cafes in the city, with good bagels *and* good coffee. So what is so damn special about this place?

Chapter 8

Ellie

As we sit in one of my favorite places in the city, I can't wait to share the experience with Reese. I have never brought anyone here before. Well, I'd brought my friends but not anyone I was interested in romantically. This is different, this is special. I have been coming here since I was a little girl and only the prices on the menu have changed. I love how much of this place is still the same as when I was younger. I order our food and return, waiting for a waitress to bring it over. I like the duality of this place, is it a cafe or a restaurant? Who knows.

"So, can I ask why this is your favorite place in the city?" Reese asks finally. I laugh because I have been waiting for it. I know it doesn't look like much, but to me it is everything.

"Yes. When I was little my grandma used to take me here. We'd walk through the city together, grab bagels and juice and sit here for hours just talking. She'd listen to me go on and on about literally anything. Here was where I decided to be a fashion designer.

She'd taken me to see a pop up museum of fashion through the years and I fell in love. She used to be a seamstress so she likes to say it was in my blood. But something clicked with me all those years ago, she was the one who encouraged me to go to college for it."

"Wow, so this place is sentimental to you becoming you," Reese says understanding.

"Yes, I know it doesn't look like much, but it's a core part of who I am. I haven't been here in a bit because my grandma doesn't get out much these days but sometimes I like to bring her bagels and we talk for hours." I smile, thinking about how I saw her just a few weekends ago. She's older and frail now, but still can talk your ear off about anything.

"I'm really glad you brought me here." Reese reaches over the table and grabs my hand. It's just enough sentiment to make me feel filled up with butterflies.

"Did I order the right thing? There were more options than I expected." Reese chuckles as the waitress brings us our food.

"I'm telling you the bagels are delicious." I ordered myself a poppy bagel with cream cheese and an iced tea.

Reese takes a bite first and I wait to see her reaction. It shouldn't matter so much if she likes the food or not, but part of me knows it is like her saying if she likes me or not. She smiles and makes an audible moan as she crunches the bacon with her bite.

"So?" I prompt after a minute. She takes a large sip of her hot tea and smiles.

"It's delicious. Definitely right about the bagels."

I smile and dig into mine. We don't talk while we

eat, which would normally make me want to say something, but today I am just happy with the silence. With Reese's presence. I've never had that before, even with my best friends, I hate an awkward silence. So this is all new territory for me. But something about the quiet is comforting for once. Like we don't have to force ourselves to find something to say every second but it isn't like we've run out of things to say either. We both are just enjoying our food and the place.

"How's your muffin?" I ask Reese and blush at how it sounds.

"It's delicious." She smirks.

"How is your food?" Reese asks.

"So good. It makes me think about when I was a kid. My grandma and I used to try everything on the menu. It took us years to get through it but I can proudly say I've tried everything at least once."

"That's awesome, I've always wanted to do that but I have trouble swaying from my usual choices." Reese shrugs.

"I was an adventurous kid. I liked trying new foods and things," I explain. Of course, I was bigger than I am now. Growing up a fat kid wasn't always the easiest, but my grandma was the one person who never made being fat seem like a bad thing. She'd always make sure I was fed and never comment on what I ate unlike my parents who tried putting me on diet after diet. It took me a long time to be comfortable in my own skin, but when I finally got there, I knew it was this fat body I felt most comfortable in.

"What are you thinking about?" Reese catches my distance.

"My grandma, she's just really ended up shaping a huge part of who I am," I explain.

"I was never close with my grandparents so it's nice to hear stories about yours. What is she like?"

"Loud and chaotic and very blunt. She's kind of like me minus the pink hair and curves. I look a lot like her though." I laugh.

"Do you have any pictures?" Reese smiles.

"I do!" I'm like a new mom excited to show pictures of their kid as I pull out my phone. Unlocking it with my face, I scroll up a bit to find pictures of my grandma and I at Shelly's a few months ago. I never know when the last time we'll be here so I always snap some photos of us, to immortalize the moment. I hate thinking like that, but better to be safe than sorry.

"Here's us, here." I scroll through a few of us smiling normally and then we put on silly snapchat filters to look like puppies.

"You both look so happy, you have the same smile," Reese points out.

"We do!" I say proudly.

"Are you an only child?" Reese asks.

"I am. Why, can you tell or something?"

"No, I'm just making conversation. There's so much I don't know about you yet."

"Well, what do you want to know?" I smile.

"Everything. But tell me something you'd only tell your best friends."

"Hmm, that's a tough one. I tend to tell them everything."

"That's why it's fun," she points out.

"You couldn't ask my favorite color or something?" I laugh.

Lucky to be Yours

"That's surface level. I want to know *you*. Like coming here obviously is special to you, do you often bring people here?"

"No." I admit. "You're the first."

"And on our first official date? I'm flattered." Reese winks and I blush.

"Oh, don't let it go to your head," I tease.

"Too late." She chuckles.

"Do you want to get out of here?"

"With you? Yes."

Reese and I bring our plates to the front, placing them on the counter basket along with the others and leave the glasses beside them. We head out the door and down the street. I take the lead again, this time deciding to walk along the city instead of taking so much of the subway. Hopefully Reese won't mind walking around but she seems to have comfortable boots on. She takes my hand again and I smile at the connection. It is a small gesture that isn't lost on me.

"So did you grow up in the city?" Reese asks the more we walk.

"Sort of. I grew up right outside the city but spent most of my time in the city growing up. I visited my grandma a lot," I explain. "Did you?"

"I actually grew up in New Jersey."

"Oh, God." I can't help myself. My distaste for New Jersey is inborn. New Yorkers are supposed to hate the state of people who think living that close to the city makes them honorary New Yorkers. Fun fact, it doesn't.

"Oh no, please tell me I didn't just ruin this," Reese says jokingly.

"I will definitely be looking at you differently now," I tease. It is too easy.

"Seriously?" She looks shocked.

"Nah, I just can't believe I'm on a date with someone from *Jersey*." I scowl after the last word for good measure.

"Hey, I mean I can go." She turns to leave, but I pull her back. Pulling Reese into me, our faces are inches apart. Suddenly nothing else seems to matter, I can't even remember what we were teasing each other about. She pushes my curls out of my face and it's like something out of a movie, she holds my face and leans in for a kiss.

Our lips burn slowly into each others. It's a sweet kiss, no tongues fighting for dominance, more of pecks keeping our lips locked together. She pulls away with a smile and I know I'm blushing. That kiss is different than our last, it feels more intimate. More *special*. I can't explain it, but it is definitely *more*.

"You're beautiful," she whispers against my lips. That's when I realize what the more is, more *intimate*. We aren't hooking up in a bathroom stall, we are kissing for the world to see and don't give two shits. It is equally terrifying and sweet.

"So are you," I whisper back.

Reese smiles and we continue on our little walk. I don't have anywhere in mind this time. I just want to walk along the city with her. Around midtown we make a few turns to avoid the end rush of the parade. It is midday and the last thing you want is to catch all the drunk idiots who are bummed the parade is over. Reese keeps her hand locked in mine and lets me lead the way which I appreciate.

"Are we going somewhere or are we just walking?" Reese asks after a bit.

"I didn't have anywhere in particular to go this time. Is that okay?" I should've asked before we started walking around aimlessly.

"That's fine, I just have to pee. Can we stop in that Starbucks?" Reese chuckles. I nod. After a quick pee and coffee stop in Starbucks, we're both ready to keep walking.

"What did you get?" I ask looking at her hot cup.

"A caramel macchiato." She looks at my iced coffee and shivers. "How are you drinking something iced?"

"It's not that cold out." I shrug and take a hearty sip.

"You're literally going to freeze your cute ass off." She chuckles.

"Then I hope you can warm it for me." I wink.

"Mmm, any day." Reese grabs a handful of my ass and squeezes. I blush because we're in public, but I am loving how affectionate she is being with me. It is so different than this morning when she didn't want to hold my hand. I am glad she feels more comfortable with me. Even just in the last few hours.

"Come on." I roll my eyes and we keep walking.

Chapter 9

Reese

The rain starts without a warning from the sky. One second it's a clear, cool, day and the next there's a huge downpour. I should've checked the weather this morning but part of me is glad I didn't. If there was a chance of this much rain, I definitely would've stayed inside today. Can you imagine? A little rain could've kept me away from seeing Ellie again. I wonder how many other missed opportunities I've had because of a little bit of weather.

"Do you want to go somewhere inside?" Ellie asks after we've been huddling under a Starbucks awning.

"Yes, do you want to come over?" I'm ready for this day to end yet.

"Like to your place?" Ellie's voice goes up an octave.

"Yes, but only if you want to. It's a few blocks that way." I point. With all the walking we've done, we ended up near my place anyway.

"Okay." Ellie smiles.

"Make a run for it?" I say, looking up at the sky. It is coming down pretty hard.

"On three." She nods.

"One..." I say.

"Two..." she says.

"Three!" we both say; holding hands we make a run for it in the direction of my apartment. It's straight down three blocks and two more over.

Despite running, we're getting soaked by the freezing rain. It is almost cold enough for this to be snow. I'm not sure which one I'd prefer in this moment. Probably the snow, then it wouldn't have soaked down to my underwear. By the time we make it to my block, I'm thankful I can see my building and I'm craving warm underwear and a nice hot shower. Maybe Ellie is craving the same.

"Reese?" a familiar voice calls and I stop running to see who it is. Under a large black umbrella is Mitchell and his new boyfriend, Anthony.

"Mitch!" I smile. He's about to reach for a hug when he sees how wet we are. Ellie and I stand under the apartment building's awning next to mine.

"Ellie, you remember my best friend Mitchell." I reintroduce them in case her memory for names is as bad as mine.

"I do! It's nice to see you."

"And I'm Anthony, Mitchell's boyfriend. Is this the famous Reese I've heard so much about?" I have only seen Anthony in Mitchell's many photos he's sent but I hadn't had the chance to meet him yet.

"Yes, guilty as charged." I laugh.

"It's nice to finally meet you." He shakes my hand and then Ellie's.

"What are you two up to?" Mitchell asks.

"Oh, well we ran into each other and we're just

hanging out," I say nonchalantly. I don't want Mitchell to say something and freak Ellie out.

"It's so nice to see the two of you together." Mitchell even adds a wink toward Ellie.

"It was quite a surprise to run into each other," Ellie says.

"Maybe it's for the best, you never know who you'll run into when you least expect it." Mitchell grins, and I feel like I'm being interviewed by my parents before prom.

"Well! We should get going, we're soaked." It sounds dirtier than I intended but standing still in the rain makes me realize how deep the rain got.

"Have fun, you two!" Mitchell calls out after us.

Ellie and I walk a few buildings down and I unlock the door for us. I am on the third floor but we take the elevator because after running in the rain there is no way I am taking the stairs too. Ellie's hair is dripping on the floor the whole elevator ride, and I try to figure out a way to politely ask her if she wants to shower. I don't think I had any dry clothes that will fit her. Maybe we should've gone to her apartment instead.

"Mitchell looked really happy with his new boyfriend," Ellie says once we step inside the apartment.

"He does, he likes him a lot," I agree.

"So, I wasn't expecting company. Sorry if my apartment is a little bit messy," I warn her as we take off our wet coats and shoes.

Looking around I think about how I should've put away my records on the table. There is a pile of dirty dishes in the sink and a ratty old blanket hanging over the couch. I start to gather some things off the floor and from around the apartment. I really should've gone to her apartment instead of mine. I'm sure hers was in prime condition.

"Hey." Ellie takes my hands as I pick up a shoe I left under my couch. "I care about hanging out with you, not what your apartment looks like."

"I'm sorry," I apologize again.

"My apartment is three times as messy which is insane because I'm like rarely home." Ellie laughs and I let my shoulders relax.

"Do you want to take a shower?"

"Excuse me?"

"Fuck, I didn't mean to sound so forward. But your hair is so wet and I don't have any dry clothes that would fit you and fuck that sounds worse-" Thankfully Ellie stops me.

"Calm down, just be yourself. There's no worry. I'd love to take a shower because I'm freezing from the rain and if you don't have anything dry then that's okay."

"I can put our clothes in the dryer downstairs. It won't take too long," I suggest, my brain finally working again. I swear she makes me more nervous than any other girl ever did.

"That would be awesome." Ellie smiles.

"My bathroom is just down the hall to the left, why don't you get undressed and just leave the clothes on the doorknob for me," I add.

"Sounds good." She nods and heads down the hallway. I pick up a few extra things around the apartment, giving her a few minutes to get undressed. Heading into my room, I quickly make the bed and grab some dry clothes for myself.

Changing into a new pair of leggings and an oversized t-shirt, I feel a lot more comfortable. I stop outside the bathroom when I hear the water for the shower running and I pick up Ellie's clothes. They're even wetter than mine somehow so I grab my laundry room key and head downstairs. I don't run into anyone and I'm back in the apartment in ten minutes. Ellie's still in the shower when I realize I forgot to give her a towel. I knock on the door a few times but over the sound of the water, it's hard to hear if she can hear me.

"El?" I call out. It sounds like she says come in so I open the door a crack, and just as I'm placing the towel on the toilet, she comes out screaming.

"Holy shit!" I close my eyes and turn around. She comes out of the bathroom a moment later in just the towel.

"If you wanted to join me you could've just said so," she teases.

"I was trying to bring you a towel so you didn't get cold," I explain.

"Oh, well how thoughtful of you." She laughs and for once in my life I think I'm actually blushing.

"So." I stand there trying not to make eye contact with her very very low hanging towel.

"Did you want to go get me my clothes?" she asks, and I nod.

"Of course!" I all but run downstairs to the laundry room and get her clothes. They're nice and dry, so I run back up to my apartment and when I get inside, Ellie is sitting on the couch in just her towel, all but lounging. It is a sexy sight.

"Thank you." She smiles.

"If I was smart, I would've lost these." I wink, holding the clothes.

"You are smart, because I definitely see them coming off again in your future." She winks and heads down the hall. On the way there she drops the towel without turning around and I admire her beautiful bare ass.

"Fuck," I mumble to myself. I am in way over my head with this woman and I can't help it. There is just something about her.

Ellie comes out a few minutes later with her pink hair tied in a bun on top of her head and dressed in just her shirt and panties. She looks sexy as hell. Like something out of a damn porno. I suddenly feel like a guy who is going to bust in ten seconds flat. She takes a seat on the couch next to me and shares the blanket I'm using. How the hell am I supposed to focus when I know she's barely dressed and less than a few inches away? I am no better than a guy.

"So, you collect records?" Ellie asks, glancing at the long wall of records and my record players. One is old and one is new, both of them playing the records differently.

"I do, I used to work in a record shop," I explain.

"That's cool, so you got most of these when you worked there?" Ellie looks from the couch. I appreciate that she isn't touching them but admiring them from afar, she must have some experience with records.

"Yeah, actually the guy who owned the place died and left me his collection. Well, half of it. The other half went to his son but I got some pretty cool ones." I point to the wall. "The ones hanging up are some of my favorites."

"Can you play one for me?"

"I'd love to." I smile. I jump up and look at the wall.

I didn't want to pick something too cheesy or too upbeat so I grab a Fleetwood Mac album and let it play. There was bound to be something good on there. It was one of my favorites.

We're both quiet as it starts to play. "Go Your Own Way" starts first, and Ellie starts to hum along with it. I am happily surprised she knows one of my favorite albums, at least one song anyway. The record plays into the next song and the next, but the more it plays, the more it becomes background music for us.

"I liked when *Glee* did the Fleetwood Mac episode," she says.

"Please tell me that's not the only reason you know these songs." I groan.

"No, my dad was a big fan. I heard them a lot growing up," she explains.

Ellie and I have gotten into a deep conversation about which episode of *Glee* was the best and why. She thinks it's the "Sexy" episode while I'm positive it's the "Blame it on the Alcohol" one. We're arguing about the song choices and how funny both are when we both start laughing. We are adults who are arguing about *Glee*. But it just feels easy and fun. With Ellie, we can talk about anything and it is simple.

"Do you want anything to drink?" I ask when I notice her Starbucks cup is empty.

"I'd love some water, thanks." She smiles and I head to my kitchen to grab us both some.

As I grabbed the glasses I can't help but think of the last time I had a woman in my apartment without the intention of having sex. Because as much as I want Ellie's body, I will be happy just sitting and talking to her for the rest of the night. Laughing about stupid things and getting to know each other more. It is like she has taken the womanizer out of me and it is terrifying. But then I think about Mitchell and how happy he is with Anthony and how long it's been since I've been happy with someone else. My hand feels wet and I'm snapped out of my thoughts as I realize I've overfilled the glass of water just a bit. I quickly pour out the excess water, fill the next cup, and hand one to Ellie.

"You okay?" She gives me a weird look as I sit back down.

"I was just thinking this was really nice." I smile.

"I thought so too." Ellie moves a little closer to me on the couch and I can feel her bare thigh pressing against my leg.

"Do you want to um... watch a movie?" I suggest quietly.

"Reese, I'd love for you to fuck me," Ellie says bluntly. There is the girl I met in the bar last year with the dirty mouth and even dirtier mind.

"Well, since you asked so nicely." I laugh and take Ellie by the hand. If we are going to have sex again, we are going to do this properly. In a bed this time.

Chapter 10

Ellie

Reese leads me to the bedroom and before I have a second to look around, her lips are pressed against mine. She puts her hands on my waist and I have mine wrapped around her neck. Our tongues dance across each other's and this time we're not fighting for dominance. She uses her top lip to pull out my bottom lip just enough to nibble it, and I groan in her mouth. I reach for the hem of her shirt but she stops me, holding back my wrists.

"I want to take this slow," she whispers.

"How slow?" I ask back. We've only been kissing and I am already dying to be touched. Something about her makes me feral when it comes to her body.

"Slow." She stops kissing me to kiss my neck, placing these achingly hot wet kisses all the way down my collarbone.

"Fuck. Slow it is," I murmur.

She runs her fingertips up and down my arms and I close my eyes, feeling how smooth her hands are. I place one hand on the small of her back as I pull her in close to me, feeling goosebumps raise on her skin. Reese's body is pressed against mine, our chests both heaving from the lack of touch. Both of us turning off our instincts to go faster and just enjoy this moment. I don't think I've ever been with someone where I wasn't trying to rip their clothes off.

Reese reaches for the hem of my shirt and slowly, achingly, she pulls it off over my head. I curse myself for putting on my bra earlier because it's just another piece she'll have to take off. As my shirt drops to the ground, she slides both of her hands down my collar bone and over my chest. She squeezes each breast in her hand, through the bra and then down my stomach. She stops to appreciate my curves, not rushing over them like past lovers have done. She stops to hold them, before venturing further down my back and to my ass. Reese squeezes lightly and pulls me in toward her. It's then I realize that the lights are still on, something that normally would bother me. But with Reese, this is all new territory.

"I want you," she whispers against my lips, and I moan. It's the first time I've heard these words from someone else and knew they had a deeper meaning.

I pull off Reese's t-shirt over her head and I stop to look her over. She's not wearing a bra so her nipples are hardened and standing at attention already, begging to be sucked on. She has a few tattoos I either didn't notice last year or she'd gotten recently. I pause as she starts kissing my neck to look at them. There's a quote on her ribs I can't make out and there's a snake on her arm with a face. No, I pause, she has a Medusa tattoo. My heart hardens as I think about its meaning. I don't ask her about it, it's not my business, but I can't help but feel bad for her. The moment passes instantly as she plucks off my bra with one hand and takes a nipple in her mouth. I couldn't focus on anything but how good her mouth feels.

Reese sucks on each nipple, palming the other with her opposite hand. While I moan and groan in euphoria. We fall backward onto the bed with a laugh and lie next to each other. I reach to push her hair out of her eyes and she holds my cheek with one hand. I close my eyes, leaning into her touch. I've never had sex like this before. So intimate. Especially with someone I like so much. Is this really what I've been missing? Giving up intimacy all those years.

I lean in to kiss her, our lips finding each other's. Her hands dancing across my body, feeling how smooth my skin is and how good she feels. My hands reach for her chest, thumbing her nipples between my fingers. I watch as she comes undone under my touch. I take it it slowly, just as she wants. I know I am teasing her more than I anticipated, but the way she moans, I can't hold back. She smells like rain and suddenly that smell is intoxicating. Everything about her is addictive.

"Touch me," she whispers, but I shake my head.

"Slowly," I whisper back, and she groans. I am already soaked, so I know how she feels but I can't help myself. I love seeing her like this.

I move so she's lying on the pillows and I'm straddling her waist, careful not to put too much weight on her. She is a small thing compared to my thick thighs. I lean down to kiss her, stopping to hold one hand on her neck while I place kisses down her collarbone, down her chest, down her stomach and right above her hipbone. I can smell her arousal and I am dying for a taste, but I pace myself. Reese bucks her hips forward and I smile as I place kisses all above her pants. Deciding to not tease her any further, I tug her pants off and she kicks them across the room. To my delight, she's not wearing any panties. Just a thin landing strip between me and her core.

"Fuck," I whimper. She has the prettiest pussy. I want to dive right in but instead I bend down and place kisses on her inner thighs. Nibbling and sucking lightly just to tease her as I get closer and closer to her core.

"Please," she whispers. I nod, knowing I've teased her long enough.

I run one finger up her wet slit, parting her lips for me. She is even wetter than I am. Holding her open, I run my tongue between her lips, licking up her juices ever so slowly. She whimpers, pushing my head down into her core, and I smile. Reese isn't someone who has to beg for it, so to see her begging is sexy as hell. To know she is dying for my touch, and my touch alone, turns me on even more.

Reese moans as I lick her pussy. I nibble gently at her clit, putting just enough pressure with my tongue to drive her wild. Looking up at her while she throws her head back in delight is one of the hottest things I've ever seen. One day I'll have to have her record it, because this is something I want to watch over and over. She pushes my head down and I flatten my tongue, pressing it to her as hard as I can, listening to her breath change and moans continue. I start slow, one lick at a time, just enough to get her wiggling under my touch for more. Then just as she's about to push me away and do it herself, I pick up the pace and listen to her body. I lick her clit and place two fingers inside her core.

"Oh! I need more!" she calls out as I pump them in and out. Listening to her, I slowly add a third finger and she groans in pleasure.

"That good, baby?" I ask, taking a break from eating her out. No one warns you how hot it gets down there. I know how to breathe from my nose but still, every once in a while I need a breath of fresh air.

"So fucking good," Reese whimpers and I duck below to continue. I want to hear her screaming my name before I stop again.

This time, I don't start slow. I pump my fingers in and out, curling them just enough to hit her g-spot and watch as she moans each time I hit it just right. When I'm sure I have a good pace, I add my tongue back in, licking her clit and sucking in all her juices. Who knew a woman could taste so damn sweet? It is like my own personal candy store and I am the only customer. I'm licking her clean when her breath gets shallow and I glance up at her.

"Oh fuck! Don't stop!" she screams, and I don't. I keep the pace, fucking her as hard as I can and she gasps, pushing my head down further into her pussy.

"Say my name," I say against her. I don't know if she can even hear me but I'm desperate for her to cry out my name.

"Oh, Ellie! Fuuuuuck!" She comes beautifully, her mouth forming this perfect O shape as she moans my name. I lick slower as she comes down, waiting for her legs to stop shaking.

"Mmm." I climb next to her in bed and lay my head on the pillow, just looking at her. Her eyes are still closed, enjoying the post orgasm haze, so I play with her hair. Twirling the pieces on the ends of my fingers.

"Fuck, you are so good at that," she murmurs after a moment. Reese runs her hand down my chest and stops just above my breasts.

"Thanks." I wink.

"I'll return the favor, just give me a second to feel my legs again." She chuckles.

"Take your time, I'm not going anywhere." I laugh. I am dying to be touched, but watching Reese need a few minutes to regain her strength is kind of hot. Knowing I did that to someone else, especially a womanizer like Reese? It is hot as hell.

"Come here." After a minute she pulls me into her, wrapping her leg around my waist. Our lips collide and I groan into her mouth as her tongue fights me for dominance. If she wants to take control, I am all for it.

Reese climbs over me and I take a moment to appreciate the view of her completely naked on top of me. God, she is fucking sexy. She takes my breasts in her hands and kneads them, playing with my nipples just enough to tease me. Then she slides her hands down my stomach, down my thighs, and grazes across my core. It's clear she's going to make this painstakingly slow for me. But I won't give her the satisfaction of begging, nope. If she wants to tease me, then fine.

"You're dying for this aren't you?" Reese smirks.

"Maybe," I allow.

"Only maybe?" She runs a hand over my panty-covered core, and I buck my hips to her touch.

"Feels like more than maybe." She smirks again. Damn her and her hotness. I am already soaked from tasting her.

Reese doesn't wait for me to answer, instead she begins kissing me. It's soft kisses that only drive me wild for her. She begins kissing down my chest, biting just rough enough for me to moan. She stops at my stomach and I think she's going to skip it all together but she surprises me by kissing it. Each inch of my stomach she grabs softly and kisses lightly. I've never had anyone do that before and it surprisingly feels good. Even just her not shying away from it is more than I can say for some. She dips under my stomach and between my thighs. She touches them, running her fingertips in my inner thighs and then presses her lips against them.

"Do you trust me?" she asks, popping her head up.

"You're not going to put a finger in my butt are you?" I ask nervously. That's usually what happens when someone asks to trust them by your nether regions.

"No, I just was going to use a toy." She chuckles. "It's clean, I only use it on myself."

"It's okay." I nod. I appreciate that she added that, I feel sort of special since she only uses it on herself.

She reaches toward her bedside table and pulls out a larger-looking red dildo. She presses a button and it comes to life. I am intrigued and turned on all at once. She dips back between my thighs and presses it lightly to my core. It is just enough to make me gasp.

"Tell me how it feels." Reese slides the toy up and down my core, soaking the toy.

"So good," I mumble.

"How about now?" Reese asks, as she dips the toy inside me I nod and she continues, putting in what feels like all of it.

"OH!" I gasp out, with the buzzing sensation and how full I feel, I am bound to be cumming soon.

"Tell me how good it feels," Reese murmurs, and

I'm breathing like all the breath has been taken away from me as she turns it up.

"Fuck. I love it." I moan. "Don't stop," I beg. Yes, Reese actually has me begging her not to stop and I don't even care. She feels so fucking good. I look down and see her perfectly round ass up in the air with a small tattoo on her backside. A black crescent moon on her left cheek. It seemed like everywhere I look she has another hidden tattoo I can find.

Reese is pushing the toy in and out of my pussy and I'm moaning, my breathing heavy when her tongue makes contact with my clit. She presses down her tongue gently and makes small circles. Reese spits and I'm surprised that I find that hot. She continues licking, and then presses her lips around it, almost as if she was kissing my clit.

"I want you to scream, don't hold back." Reese pushes up to speak. I nod but she smirks. "Use your words, baby." She pauses. "Or I stop." The toy turns off and I gasp in frustration.

"I'll scream," I moan out. "But don't stop."

She smirks, turning the toy back on but this time up even higher. "Ah! Yes!" I call out. If she wants me to be vocal, I won't hold back.

"That's perfect, baby," she says again but this time I smile. I love the use of pet names, and honestly hearing her call me baby makes me even wetter.

"Mmm," I groan as she moves the toy even harder in and out of me.

"Right there, baby," she says before putting her tongue back to work. She uses small circles to build me up and with the toy filling me completely I can feel my orgasm rising. Heavy breaths take over as I can feel myself cumming around the toy. I close my thighs, crushing Reese's head in-between them.

"Yes! Oh! Yes! Fuck!" I'm screaming as loud and can be and she's not letting up. I finally have to tap her out, releasing my thighs as I fall back into her pillows.

"Damn." Reese turns off the toy, throws it aside, and lies down next to me.

"Mmm," I agree, unable to really speak. That felt so fucking amazing.

Reese looks at me, her eyes on my lips as the corners of her mouth turn up. She's looking at me differently than before. I'm sure it's a good thing, but intimacy could kiss me on the mouth and I'd have no idea what it looked like. It has been too long since I've had any. But if it comes with the way she is looking at me and the way I feel, maybe I won't mind having it again.

Chapter 11

Reese

We lie next to each other in silence after what can only be described as mind blowing sex. I lay on my side looking at Ellie for a while but when she doesn't speak, I lay on my back looking up at the ceiling. It feels a little bit awkward, but I don't know what to say to make it feel not awkward. I'm not used to this, normally after sex I make some kind of excuse or take a shower and hope they'll be gone by the time I get out. But Ellie is different. For the first time ever, I don't want her to be gone. It feels like a long time before either of us speak. When we do, Ellie's the first to say something.

"So... awkward silence," she says with a laugh, and I can't help but laugh too.

"I didn't know what to say," I admit.

"Me either." She turns on her side to face me so I do the same.

"I'm not used to anyone sticking around for conversation after sex, but I didn't want you to go." I figure if Ellie could break the silence, I should admit that.

"Oh my gosh, same here! I was hoping you'd let me stay." She smiles.

"Trust me, I'd love to do that again but I need a nap first, so you're more than welcome to stay." I laugh.

"A nap right now sounds fantastic." Ellie groans.

"Well, if you make sounds like that, a nap might not happen." I wiggle my eyebrows and lean in for a kiss.

"No no, you said nap and I'm-" She stops to yawn. "Very exhausted."

"Okay, baby." The name slips off my tongue just like before, but this time I see her blush.

Ellie leans into me and I wrap my arms around her. Pulling the sheets over us, we lie together in my bed. Ellie closes her eyes and I run my fingers down her bare shoulders, rubbing slowly. She yawns again and I realize I'm putting her to sleep but she doesn't complain. Somewhere between her soft sighs, the shoulder rubs, and my own yawns, we both fall asleep.

I wake to Ellie's eyes on me. It slightly startles me, forgetting for a moment that there was someone else in my bed, but when I remember it's Ellie, I'm instantly calm. In our sleep we must have moved around a lot because now Ellie is holding my hands and we are facing each other again.

"Good afternoon, sleepyhead." She smiles and bites her bottom lip.

"Hey." I yawn and smile back at the beautiful woman in my bed.

"You're cute when you sleep." Ellie whispers and leans in for a quick kiss.

"Stop, I probably look like an alien," I complain.

"Nope, you're cute," she insists so I roll my eyes. A

soft breeze blows from the door, and it becomes apparent of how naked we are.

"Did you want to do it again?" Ellie asks with a wiggle of her eyebrows.

"Is that even a question?" I wink, and Ellie climbs on top of me to start kissing me. Her thighs touch mine, and I can feel she's already soaked in anticipation.

"Fuck, baby, is all that for me?" I ask running two fingers up her slit.

"Well, I would hope so." She moans.

"You like it when I call you baby?" I ask as I palm her clit and she gasps.

"I do, I fucking do," she moans out, and I smile. There is nothing hotter than having a woman in complete control under your touch. "Does it mean something?"

"What?" I drop my hand and look at her.

"Does it mean something to call me that? Or is that just like a turn on?"

"Are you trying to ask me what we are?" I raise an eyebrow at her.

"No, because that would be cliche and needy as hell. I don't need to know what we are." She shrugs on top of me.

"You don't?"

"Nope." She looks convincing, but I've been with enough women to know they always want to know what we are. But for once I don't mind the woman who is asking it and for once, I have an answer.

"Are you sure? Because I have an answer for you." I chuckle. I can't help it, she is so fucking cute when she pouts.

"You do?" She uncrosses her arms and looks at me surprised.

"I do," I say softly.

"What's that?" She turns, waiting for me to reply.

"Ha! I knew you wanted to know."

"That was SO mean!" She slides off my lap, but I pull her back in and we're a tangle of body parts as I kiss her and she laughs.

"I don't do relationships well," I admit. If I am going to start something with Ellie, I need her to know the truth, to know how things really are and why I am the way I am.

"I don't either." She sighs. We both sit up, naked and vulnerable, and I decide this is the moment I want to tell her about my past.

"I've never been in a relationship that wasn't toxic, and I don't mean just bad and using the word toxic for fun but I mean actually toxic. I'm a survivor, and relationships have never been easy for me which is why I gave them up for a long time." I have never told anyone besides Mitchell about this, but it just seems right. I know Ellie isn't going to judge me for it.

"I noticed your Medusa tattoo, I wasn't going to ask unless you brought it up first," she admits. I nod. It was something I took a long time to get, wanting something to signify the strength of what I went through and knowing I'm a survivor because of it, not a victim.

"I just have a hard time seeing the good in people and believing they'll stay good when I've seen time and times again how people actually are."

"I would never hurt you." Ellie takes my hand. "But I don't want to make promises without knowing your story. Or diminishing it, so I'm here to listen. I'm not judging your past or you."

"I just need you to know that I'm terrified of the risks, but I do like you. More than I intended to."

"I like you too." She smiles. I've been so wrong about relationships but as I sit here with Ellie, I can't help but wonder if maybe that was because I hadn't found the right person yet. I've never felt comfortable enough to tell anyone else what I've been through, but here I am telling Ellie everything. It all slides out like butter on a pan, with no remorse or fear.

"Maybe we can take this slow, and just see how it goes," I suggest.

"Slow seems to be our thing," she says with a light laugh.

"Is that okay?" I ask anxiously. Maybe she wants something more than I can give her right now. It is just hard to jump so fast into things when I am always worried the past was my fault. Despite somewhat knowing that it wasn't, it's hard not to feel like some of what happened to me was my fault. It doesn't make it right, but feelings aren't facts. Something I try to remind myself of often.

"It's more than okay, I'm just getting back into things. I know that I like you and being with you, so for now, slow is perfect." She leans in to slowly kiss my lips. She draws out my tongue, slowly sucking on it, and I moan in her mouth.

"Fuck." I can't help myself. Ellie is sexy as hell and knows all the right buttons to push when it comes to my body.

"You don't have to do this you know, you can think about what I said, or you can go. I know it was a lot."

"Reese, will you let me kiss you? Because right now I want to show you I'm not going anywhere. I'm ready to jump in and take things as slow as you need."

"Really?" It slips from my mouth before I can think about it.

"Yes, really. I'd love to show you what a non toxic relationship can be like." Ellie holds my jaw in her hand, and I nod. Letting her know she can kiss me.

She traces her thumb over my bottom lip. I pretend to bite her, and she laughs. Moving her thumb, she holds my face and leans in to kiss me fully. Her lips melting into mine, our tongues colliding, and her body climbing onto mine. She straddles me and I reach for her chest, her large breasts barely fitting in my hands. I take her nipples between my fingers and tug enough to elicit a moan from her lips. I love how sensitive she seems to be.

"Touch me," I whisper into her lips.

Ellie reaches for my neck, wrapping her manicured hand around my throat and squeezing. I gasp, why the hell is choking so hot? I don't care, her hands leave my neck and her lips find my breasts, sucking on my nipples rough enough to leave behind marks. Is she branding me? I have never been into hickies before but the thought of her staying on me all day is enough to make me wetter.

"I want you," Ellie whispers.

"I want you too," I whisper back.

Ellie slides between my thighs, her tongue connecting with my core feels like heaven. I close my eyes, wanting to commit as much of this to memory as possible. Her rough fingertips on my thighs, her warm breath on my core, the way her tongue presses itself against me. I bite down on my bottom lip, trying to keep my moans at bay. Ellie works her way through my core, her tongue flattening, licking, and sucking to make me dripping at her touch.

"I want to use your toy on you," Ellie says, sitting up.

"Okay." I nod. I reach for it on the nightstand and hand it to her. I wonder if she is going to tease me with it like I teased her. I shiver in anticipation of whatever she is going to do to me.

"I want you to moan and not hold back, it's me. Be yourself," she whispers, and I smile. It is surprisingly easy to be myself with Ellie. I'm not worried about her judgements because I know she doesn't have any. She is just here with me and lets me be myself.

"Okay, baby." I kiss her lips softly until she pulls away.

She turns on the toy with one hand, putting it on the lowest setting. The dull vibrations shaking her hand as she lowers the toy between us. Running it up and down my slit, as slow as possible, I feel myself growing wetter. I was right, she is going to tease me.

"Oh," I breathe out a light moan. I keep my eyes open, wanting to anticipate her next moves.

Ellie takes one hand and brushes her thumb across my bottom lip, down across my jawline and tugs on my hair. It's just long enough to grab ahold of. She pulls my head forward so she can kiss me while keeping the toy between my legs, pushing it against my clit.

"Turn it up," I mumble and she nods, fumbling with the buttons. She clicks it up once more, letting the buzzing get louder and the intensity larger. My breath hitches as it connects with my clit again and she moves it slowly across my core.

"How's that feel?" She smirks, knowing what it's doing to me.

"Mmm, it would feel better inside me," I tell her. She wants me to be honest so I'm not holding back anymore. She nods again and moves only the toy to put it inside me. I loudly gasp as she puts the toy inside me fully. I should've expected it, but fuck does it feel good.

"Better?" Ellie asks as she moves it in and out of me.

"Y-yes." I stumble over my words because it feels so good. I can feel it sliding in and out of me while Ellie leans in to start kissing my neck again. She nibbles harder and harder, definitely leaving a mark on me. It feels way too fucking good to ask her to stop. One of Ellie's hands makes its way to my breast, her thumb and pointer finger taking my nipple between them and tugging. I clench my jaw but remember what she said.

"Oh fuck!" I call out. If she wants vocal, she'll get every moan and sound I usually hold back.

"That's my girl," she whispers heavily in my ear. I don't know what turns me on more, her words or her actions.

"Please don't stop," I whisper back. I can feel my orgasm building, the infinite stars are just moments away if she keeps up what she is doing, and I hope she does.

Ellie goes back to sucking on my neck, tugging on my nipple, and pushing the toy inside me. How she manages to do all three things at once is something I'll have to ask her later because I don't want her to stop. Everything feels so fucking good, it's like a sensory overload as she touches me. My breath hitches, letting out a few deep moans as I struggle to keep my eyes open as the orgasm hits me.

"I'm coming! Oh god, yes! Don't stop!" I scream out. Moans and my legs shake as I experience one of the best orgasms I've ever had. There is a reason that is one of my favorite toys. It know what it is doing but add in the girl of my dreams, and I am set.

I collapse into the bed, finally closing my eyes, and I feel lips pressing against mine. It's light, just enough to get a peck out of me. I can feel her smiling against me, and I smile too. She extends her arms and I lean in. I will be the last to admit it, but I live for this with Ellie. The aftermath of sex, of cuddling with her in her arms. I love just being next to her after feeling so close to her. We pull the sheets over us and she begins to twirl my hair, a sign that she is ready for another nap. I laugh to myself, this is what our life is now. Sleep and sex with the girl I really like. Could it really be this easy? I have never experienced a person who made me feel so safe and secure in such a short period of time. Letting my guard down in so many ways. Ellie's lips find my forehead, as if to reassure my thoughts I'm not saying aloud. Just to let me know, this is good, we are good.

Chapter 12

Ellie

When I wake up the next day in Reese's bed, it takes me a moment to get my bearings. Reese is sprawled out next to me, lying on her stomach with her ass exposed, so I enjoy the view for a moment. I must've taken all the sheets sometime in the middle of the night but I am surprised she hasn't fought me for them back. I unwrap myself a little and place some over her. She moves slightly but doesn't wake up so I keep admiring her. The sun is coming in from the window above us and she is illuminated by the light. Reese is always beautiful but with this lighting, she looks god-like.

"Hey." I poke Reese's shoulder and she stirs for a moment before yawning and turning to face me.

"Mmm, good morning." She opens her eyes slightly and smiles. I am relieved she is happy to see that I am still here. After last night we kind of fell asleep and when I woke to pee at 3am I was too exhausted to wake her and go home on my own. I didn't think she'd mind if I stayed, but the reassurance is nice.

"Good morning." I lean in to kiss her head. My breath smelling morning like, and I'm sure hers does too. We hadn't left this bed in almost two days now, and I am suddenly aware of things like needing to shave and brushing my teeth.

"What time is it?" she mumbles.

I reach and glance at my phone which has been on do not disturb for longer than it's ever been before. "Ten thirty-two."

"Hmm." She pauses. "Would you like to grab some brunch with me?"

"You mean leave your apartment?" I feign a gasp.

"Yes, I thought we could go on an actual date that doesn't take place in my bed." She laughs.

"I'd love that." I smile. "But could we shower first?"

"Of course." She nods. Reese sits up in bed and stretches her arms, the blanket falling to her waist, giving me a good look at her chest. Mmm, how I'd love to have those in my mouth again. But there'll be time for that later. Right now I am in desperate need of a shower and some toothpaste.

"Will you join me?" I ask hesitantly. I know some people don't like showering together but it is one of my favorite things to do with another person.

"I'd love to." She smiles.

We head to the bathroom, Reese grabbing clothes, and I realize I'll have to wear the St. Patricks day outfit I came in. I'm going to look like I haven't left her apartment in days, which is true but I don't necessarily want to look the part. Reese grabs me an extra toothbrush she got from the dentist and we brush our teeth together first. It is cute how domestic we are being, like it is just normal for us. She turns the water on and gets in first, and let me tell you just when I thought she couldn't get any hotter, I was wrong. Wet Reese is a hundred times hotter than dry Reese. She's sexy and dripping like something out of a porno and I can't help but smile that she's all mine.

Last night was a lot. I knew Reese had been through some stuff but it meant a lot that she shared it with me. Going slow with her is a lot better than rushing into anything anyway, I am just dipping my toes back into dating. Not that I will be dating anyone else, but I am happy to see where it will go with her. Things with Reese just feel *simple*. There aren't complications or big scary things in the way, it doesn't even feel like there is much of a choice when it comes to us. It just feels like this is how things are meant to be. Which feels cheesy as hell so there is no way I'll say that aloud, but I am happy taking things slow with her.

I step into the shower with her and pull down my hair from its messy bun. Reese picks up a bit of shampoo and tells me to turn around. She gets my hair wet and then starts massaging in the shampoo, gently rubbing circles in my scalp, it feels like a massage. It is some kind of magic her fingers can work. She runs her fingers through my long curls and scrunches, making sure to cover every inch with soap before taking the hose and massaging it through, to release the soap. It feels even better than when the hairdresser does it at the hair salon.

I turn around and Reese hands me a soapy loofah. I run it across her collarbone, from one side to the other and then down and around her breasts. I rub it across her arms, her stomach, and then back across her chest. She turns around, and I make sure to get every inch of her muscular back. She must work out or something because she has some serious back muscles.

"Do you work out?" I ask aloud.

"I do." She laughs. "Not much, but I like to go a few times a week."

"Well, your back looks amazing," I say admiringly.

"Thank you." She takes the loofah from me and picks up a soapy washcloth.

Reese runs it across my chest, my shoulders, my arms. She rubs slow circles across every inch of my body as I close my eyes and take in how good this feels. I swear it is going to put me back to sleep with how relaxing it is. More sensual than sexual, she is getting to know my body more intimately. She stops over my stomach and just like during sex, she doesn't hide or brush over my curves, she enjoys them. Every inch of my stomach is soaped and massaged just like the rest of me. I turn around as she washes my back, she even slides down and grabs my ass. Sliding her hands around me, she drops the washcloth and reaches for my breasts. Her naked body pressed against my back, I moan softly as she touches me.

I turn around, letting our soapy bodies collide into one. Our lips doing the same. We're suddenly in a frenzy, feeling the sexual tension build. I want her as close to me as possible, and I can tell she wants the same. I slide a hand between her thighs and she groans. It is clear we are going to make this a very dirty shower. Our hands doing all the work, we build each other up, letting the orgasms crash at the same time. Which is a little bit dangerous as we both almost fall into each other.

"We're going to miss brunch," Reese says as the water starts to run cold.

"We should get going then." I wink and we rinse off quickly. Reese hands me a fresh towel and I pad into her room to get dressed, with her close behind.

I slide into my old clothes, while Reese slides into some ripped jeans and a white t-shirt. I wonder if that is her usual attire of choice. I haven't seen her much with her clothes on yet. We both slide on our shoes and jackets and head outside. It occurs to me that I don't even know what the weather will be like. It is March in New York which literally means it can be anywhere from freezing and snowing to warm and not needing a jacket. Winter in New York is weird as hell. Thankfully, when we step outside it is cool enough to need a jacket but not freezing where my legs will be cold from the lack of clothing.

"Do you have somewhere in mind for brunch?" I ask as we step outside. Reese looks at her phone and starts leading the way.

"I do! I have this place I've been wanting to try that's not too far." She smiles. I take her hand and she tightens her fingers around mine.

By the time we get to the place, five blocks later, it's busy but we put our name down and wait outside.

"I'm sorry, I should've realized we'd need a reservation."

"Hey, I don't mind waiting." I smile. I hadn't even realized it was Sunday until I overheard someone else say it. I lost all track of time being with her.

We get called shortly anyway and we're taken to a booth on the second floor. The place is nice, it reminds me of the bar we went to last year where we played pool together for the first time. There's a long bar across one wall and the other is a wall full of booths filled with people eating brunch. Everything looks and smells good as we pass by it. My stomach grumbles in anticipation.

"Order whatever you want, it's on me." Reese smiles.

"Are you sure?" I feel weird about people paying for things for me.

"It's a date, I asked you out. I'd like to pay." Reese nods.

"Okay."

I look over the menu and everything sounds just as good as to be expected. Reese didn't know when she asked, but I freaking love brunch. The mimosas, the breakfast and lunch foods combined? Absolute perfection. I am always begging my friends to go out for brunch on the weekends.

"Can I get you anything to start?" the waitress asks, coming over. She smiles at Reese and as much as I want to mark my territory, I realize Reese hasn't even noticed her. Reeses' eyes are on me as she waits for me to place my drink order.

"Um, just the unlimited mimosas please."

"Ooo, that sounds good, can you make that two?" Reese smiles at me.

"Sure." The waitress looks a little tiffed that Reese didn't so much as glance in her direction. I'm not normally one to be jealous, actually that's not true. I am one hundred percent the jealous type and it is only a matter of time before I make it clear Reese and I are here together, as on a date. But something about Reese makes me feel like that isn't necessary, like I don't need to mark my territory with her, because she isn't going anywhere. It is a weird and good feeling to have.

"What are you going to get?" Reese asks, putting down her menu.

"The berry French toast sounds good but so does the buffalo chicken dip." I had been eyeing both of them.

"Let's get both, I'll split the buffalo dip with you if that's okay."

"Sounds perfect." I nod.

The waitress comes back with a pitcher of mimosas, two champagne glasses, and takes our food order. She's less obvious about her little crush on Reese, but mine grows bigger when Reese orders for me. I thought that would be something rude, but she orders everything the way I want and even folds my menu for me.

"So are you still working as a barista?" I ask, realizing I don't know what she does for a living.

"I am, but I've been taking night classes at BMCC a few times a week to get my bachelor's degree," she says proudly.

"What are you getting your degree in?"

"Music. There's a lot of different jobs I could have with it, so I've been enjoying learning which ones I might like the best." She smiles.

"I love that, are there any you're leaning toward?"

"I have considered being a music teacher, but I'm not so sold on the idea of working with little kids," Reese admits.

"Yeah, I don't blame you. I don't know how Morgan does it. She's a third grade teacher now and loves it, but I couldn't spend my day around such small children." I shake my head.

"It's definitely not for everyone," she agrees. "Are you still working for that boss you hate?"

"Kind of, I work for her but on a very distant basis. I actually design my own clothes now and have a few pieces in a few stores here in the city," I say proudly. It was a recent contract where I design for a few of the bigger name stores with my name on the designs, so it is still surreal to me.

"Wow, that's so exciting! Is it like contract based or was it a one time deal?"

"I'm contracted to a few different places so I design pieces for different lines and shops, depending on their needs."

"That's really so cool, you'll have to show me your designs sometime."

"Really?" I choke on the mimosa I am sipping.

"Of course, either at the stores or your sketch books or whatever. It would be cool to see your process and then the finished pieces."

"I'd love that." I smile. No one I've dated has ever been interested in my designing process before. Even my friends find it a little boring. They'll let me talk about it but I know it isn't something they are super interested in.

The waitress delivers the buffalo chicken dip and chips, and it smells as good as it looks. I reach for a chip and get a good amount of dip, letting the cheese dangle from the chip as I quickly push it into my mouth. It's a little hot but not enough to burn me thankfully. Reese grabs a chip and does the same. We're both too involved in the dip to continue taking, but the silence isn't deafening. It's a nice break with silence that's welcomed from both of us.

Reese sips her mimosa as I pour myself a second one. They are limited to an hour and I want to get my money's worth. Well, Reese's money worth. Reese chugs down the rest of hers and tips her glass toward me to pour her another.

"Hey, I gotta keep up." She chuckles.

"It's not a race, babe." I don't know where the babe comes from but I like the way it sounds. And from the blush on Reeses face, I can tell she likes it too.

"Well, we can't have you drunk at brunch and me sober." She laughs.

"Very true, drink up." I pour her a little more on the top.

Our food comes out and everything is just as good as the buffalo chicken dip. Reese gets these chocolate chip pancakes she insists on sharing, and I give her a few bites of my French toast. I'm pretty sure we're turning into one of those gross couples but I don't seem to care as much as I thought I would. By the time brunch is over, we're both mimosa drunk and stumbling on the way to my apartment. Reese insists on walking me home even though it's all the way uptown and she's only a few blocks away. I'd stay at Reese's place another night but I am desperate for some new clothes and a night of sleep in my own bed. Not that the thought of drunk sex with Reese in my bed sounds like the worst idea.

Chapter 13

Reese

Brunch with Ellie went better than I could've thought. Although maybe it only feels that way because we're both totally wasted. Nope. It really did go well because even when it's quiet with Ellie, it doesn't feel silent. Like we can sit in this comfortably and know we're thinking about the other. It's this weird thing I've never experienced with any of my exes. We're stumbling on our way to Ellie's apartment, hand in hand. Her hand always feels a little sweaty but I wouldn't tell her that because my hands are always cold.

"These shoes are *killing* my feet," Ellie exclaims suddenly. I glance down at her high heeled boots and then back at my feet.

"What size are you?"

"Um, seven?"

"Me too, want to swap?"

"You'd do that?!" she exclaims happily.

"Of course." I shrug. We lean against the building we're near and swap shoes. I'm wearing a pair of comfortable converse so she slips them on and audibly moans which does things to my nether region.

"Well, this will be fun," I say aloud and slip on her shoes. I stand up and I'm a bit wobbly, from the champagne or the shoes is unclear. Probably the combination of both. I'm not a heel person in any realm, but I want my girl to be comfortable.

"Are you okay?"

"Are you?" Is what really matters.

"I am, my feet thank you." She smiles. I lean in to kiss her, and she presses her lips to mine.

We continue walking, she holds my arm this time to steady me and after a few blocks I understand why she didn't want to wear these. They are hard as hell on my feet, but I don't make a face about it. I'll just soak my feet when I get home later and call it a night.

"Oh my gosh!" Ellie gets excited and lets go of me, forgetting she's steadying me.

"What?" I hold her shoulder and look up at the sign she's staring at. It's for an adult entertainment store; a sex toy shop.

"Oh." I start to blush, and she giggles.

"Can we go in?"

"Uh, sure?" I don't know what exactly she is looking for in there but I love the idea of looking at stuff with her. I am pretty adventurous in the bedroom and I have the feeling Ellie is too.

"Yay!" She claps and opens the door.

Inside it is bright and open, the complete opposite of the dark front doorway. There is a guy in his mid-twenties sitting behind a clear desk of sex toys. He is playing on his phone, looks up I assume to see if we're of age, and then goes back to his game. Ellie and I shrug,

Lucky to be Yours

and she leads me to the back of the store. The guy glances in our direction but doesn't seem to care enough. Besides the place is covered in security cameras and mirrors wherever you look.

"Look." She points at the wall of dildos in front of us, giggling.

"Baby." I laugh. She is clearly too drunk to be adult about this.

"They're just so *big*." She makes arm gestures at one that looks as big as her arm.

"Who can even *fit* these?" I wince. There is no kink judgement, just general curiosity about how that even works. Like technically.

"I don't know." She looks as worried as I do.

"What are we here for, baby?" I ask.

"Maybe one of those?" She points and bites her bottom lip nervously. God, she is so cute but I brace myself before looking at what she's pointing at.

"Oh! A strap on? Hell fucking yes." I nod. I've topped girls with one before but I am a big believer in everyone having their own strap so it went when the girl did.

"I want to top you." She wiggles her eyebrows, and I pick up the box with the pink one. It is eight and a half inches which seems like a good size.

"Wait, me?" I had assumed I'd be the one topping her.

"Yes, I want to fuck you." She bites her bottom lip and I'm dying to bite it for her. I lean in, our bodies pressing together. We're about to start kissing when I remember the guy in the front. I'm sure he can see from every angle and I don't want to give him a free show.

"Well, that was a tease." Ellie groans, but I tilt my head toward the guy.

"Oh." She nods and widens her eyes, making it a lot more obvious than intended.

"Back to you trying to top me." I nod.

"Really?" Ellie smiles, and I laugh. It is surprisingly easy to keep my girl happy.

"OH my gosh, look at this!" She's pointing to the old porn on the wall. Full of guys with huge dicks but with mustaches and mullets to show their ages. It is kind of gross, but she picks up one with a woman on it and we both glance through the 1950s of breasts.

"Is there anything else you wanted to get?" I ask.

"No, well we don't need condoms or lube." She twists her mouth as if she's thinking about what else we might need.

"Bondage?" She holds up a feathery pair of handcuffs and I grimace.

"I don't like being restrained," I explain. I expect her to ask why but she just nods and puts them back on the shelf. I smile, I am so relieved to have someone who understands my boundaries and respects them so naturally. It is something I am not used to yet.

"Nipple clamps?" She holds some up.

"Now that I'm into." I wink and take them from her.

Ellie continues on the store, looking everything over so she's sure not to miss anything, and I follow behind her happily. I carry the strap on and the nipple clamps around, and I realize this is what it's going to be like shopping with her. She looked so cute as she touches the sexy costumes and sits on the sex chair. Well, before the guy tells us we aren't allowed to sit on it.

"They don't have anything for anyone bigger than a size four." Ellie sighs, pawing through the lingerie.

"That's stupid." I frown. "You should make a line of sexy plus size lingerie."

Ellie freezes, staring at me.

"What?" For a moment I worry about my words, were the words plus size suddenly offensive? I didn't mean them in a negative way. *Fuck, I hoped she isn't upset.*

"That's a brilliant idea."

I let go of all the air in my body I was holding in.

"They really don't have enough out there, and they could always use more." I shrug.

"That's so true, it's really a great idea." Ellie grabs my face and plants a huge kiss on me. I see the guy in the back of one mirror smirking at us.

"Okay, it's time to go now," I decide. We pay, well, I pay because it's like buying a woman flowers, she shouldn't have to pay for her own sex toys.

"Want to come back to my place and try these out?" Ellie asks once we get outside. I'm stumbling again, the floor much less even outside than it was inside with these boots. Ellie steadies me and smiles.

"I'd love to." I bite my bottom lip and lean in for a kiss. Her lips are sweet and soft, tasting like maple syrup leftover from brunch.

We keep walking, Ellie holding me as we make our way to the subway. We opt for the elevator, thanks to Ellie's shoes, and make our way to the platform. The train comes quickly and we're only on it a few stops before Ellie says it's time to get off. She's as drunk as I am so I'm hoping she knows which stop is hers and isn't sending us on some wild goose chase.

"Here we are." She pulls out a small silver key from her jean skirt pocket and unlocks the front of her brownstone. Once we're safely inside her apartment, I kick off her boots and line them up next to the front door where the rest of her shoes are thrown about.

"I don't know how you survived the other day in those shoes, we walked all over and you didn't say a word."

"I was trying to impress you," she admits.

"What?"

"Yeah, I didn't want you to think I wanted to go home or cut the date short so I just carried on," she admits.

I wobble over to her, with my now swollen feet and hold her face in my hands. "You never have to do things like that to impress me. You impress me by being yourself."

Ellie responds by pushing her lips on mine, and we stumble into the hallway of her apartment. Our drunken stumbles are only amplified by Ellie's messy apartment, she's right it is messier than mine. Because one wrong turn on a sneaker and we'd both go flying.

"Come here." Ellie pulls me by the hand into her bedroom and our lips crash into each other. It's different than before, similar to our first time at the bar. We are both drunk and want each other faster than our clothes can come off.

ELLIE

I'm still holding the bag of sex stuff so I throw it on the bed and Reese's lips are on my neck. I tilt my head so she can get a better angle and her teeth nibble on my neck, reaching my earlobe and then back to my neck. Something that shouldn't feel so sexy but does.

"Get these off." I want her naked and touching me like hours ago, so I pull at her clothes. She giggles and steps back to get undressed, leaving me to do the same. It is just easier to get undressed yourself.

I throw my clothes to the ground, happy to be free of them and crawl into the bed, slowly letting her stare at my ass while I get in.

"Mmm, what a tease," she mumbles and climbs behind me. Suddenly there's a loud slap and her hand is on my ass.

"Oh!" I gasp, surprised by the contact.

"So fucking hot," she murmurs and comes up behind me. She lifts her hand and again slaps my ass with just enough force to drive me wild. It is like the good kind of pain.

"Lay down," I tell her, and she nods. Climbing into my bed, she lays down on the pillows and waits for further instruction. I can tell she must be horny because one hand is achingly close to her pussy, probably dying to touch it.

I pick up the bag of things and unpack the strap on first. I tear open the box and pull out the pink, plastic, lifelike piece. Figuring I should probably clean it first, I head to the bathroom, following the directions on the box and dry it with a towel. On my way back to the room, I hear Reese's sexy moans and my pussy starts to drip. *Is she fucking herself in my bed?* Because if so, that is hot as fuck.

I walk into my bedroom and find Reese, two fingers deep in her own pussy, her eyes closed and feeling herself. I let out a shallow breath and her eyes pop open.

"I couldn't wait." She smirks.

"Mm, then please don't stop, babe." I nod. It is like my own personal show and I don't want it to end. She slides her fingers up and around her clit, rubbing soft circles and then back into her pussy they go. Disappearing and reappearing as she pumps them in and out of her dripping core. I am dying for a taste but I want to watch this first.

"Help me?" she whispers, and I nod. I slide my body over to hers and start sucking on her breasts. One nipple in my mouth and the other between my fingers is enough to speed up her hands. She's pumping them even faster now, and her breath is rough as she continues.

"I want you to make yourself cum," I whisper in her ear. Reese bites her bottom lip and nods, she puckers her lips asking for a kiss and I comply. Holding her face in my hands and kiss her with all that I got, while her hands are working their magic between her thighs. But after a few minutes she pulls away and moans.

"Oh fuck!" She calls out, her hands moving as fast as they can. I pull back, so I can watch. Leaving my hands on her breasts, I watch her face as she locks eyes with me and her orgasm takes over. Her legs are shaking and her hand is dripping with her juices but god if she doesn't look sexy as hell when she comes.

"Wow," I whisper with a smile. I kiss her cheek lightly, giving her a minute to catch her breath. I pull away to put on the strap on and get myself ready because all I wanted to do now was make her cum all over again.

"Are you ready?" I ask, making sure she's still okay with this.

"Yes, but I want a safe word in case I want to stop," she says sitting up.

"Of course, what's the word?"

"Umm, red?"

"Okay, red means stop so that makes sense." I nod. She lays back down and I position myself between her thighs. I'd topped some women before but I had a feeling it wasn't going to be anything like this.

Moving my hips, I slowly enter Reese. She is clearly wet enough from her own playing so I slide right in. Reese gasps as I do, filling her up and leaning over her to steady myself. I lean in to kiss her, and she bites my bottom lip, causing a little moan from me. But it's when I kneel on my knees and start moving my hips that she begins really moaning.

"Oh! Fuck, that feels so good," she gasps. I hold her leg on my shoulder and watch as her small tits begin to bounce with each thrust inside her.

"Mmm, you like that?" I smirk. I knew she'd like being topped. Everyone loves being taken care of at some point, and knowing Reese, she's probably never trusted anyone enough to let them do this. It's not lost on me how much this probably means to her.

"I do," she gasps as I buck my hips harder.

"Turn over," I command, and she nods.

I pull out gently, and she groans at the lack of it but does what I say. Getting on her knees, she lays down and sticks her beautifully round ass in the air. Giving me a better look at that tattoo I noticed earlier. The black crescent moon is just an outline on her butt cheek but it suits her. Sliding back inside her, Reese moans and I begin moving my hips even faster. Holding onto hers for support as I slide in and out of her. I am dripping wet, I can't wait to be touched after this. But the more I pleasure Reese, the more I get turned on. I need to make her cum again. She slides a hand between her legs and starts playing with her clit.

"I want you to make yourself cum again, babe," I whisper, leaning down as close as I can get to her ear.

"Yes, baby," she gasps, and I reach for her chest. Palming her breasts with one hand, keeping my pace steady, sends her over the edge. Reese's legs begin to shake, her body stiffens, and she calls out my name with a loud moan.

"Yes, keep going," I whisper. I want to see her begging me to stop.

"Oh! Oh! Okay! Red!" she gasps after a moment, and I pull out immediately.

"You okay?" I look at her worried, turning her body over.

"I'm so good, I just couldn't cum anymore." She giggles.

"Oh." I breathe a sigh of relief. I was worried I hurt her or something.

"Give me a minute, take that off, and it's your turn with that." She smirks.

"I like the sound of that."

Chapter 14

Ellie

Reese and I become somewhat inseparable in our first few weeks of dating. Not in the bad and toxic way, but more in the we don't want to leave each other's side way. Reese stayed over the first few nights until our week day schedules became too busy to keep entertaining each other. Plus we weren't getting enough sleep when the other was over. It was kissing or talking until five am and we'd start our days on two hours of sleep. Something I never thought I'd get to do with someone else again. Reese was just so easy to be with, it didn't make things complicated or stress me out. The two of us could just be. Which is how I ended up missing a few visits of seeing my grandmother.

On our three week anniversary, Reese and I were in bed when my phone rang with a call from her. She was hoping I'd bring her something from Shelly's and come for a visit. As much as I didn't want to, I didn't want to neglect anyone for my new relationship. So I kicked Reese gently out of my bed and made my way downtown. I grabbed my grandmother her favorite sandwich, a cranberry orange muffin, and a cup of tea.

"Well, look who it is," my grandma exclaims as I walk in.

"Turn down the volume on your hearing aid, Grandma." I make a gesture with my ear, but she waves me off. Coming in close to give me a big hug.

"Oh stop, give me a hug."

Grandma's apartment is a cute studio apartment that she leased fifty years ago and refuses to move out of. Her bed is in the living room but she doesn't care, she says it makes the place more cozy when she watches television. The kitchen is next to the bathroom, which is less than ideal, but at least she has enough of a view of the city that it doesn't matter. The window beside her bed is floor to ceiling of beautiful stained glass window. It was always my favorite thing about her apartment growing up because it looks like something out of a princess castle.

"Here's your food." I take a seat at the kitchen table she has and shrug off my coat. My grandma puts the food on the counter and places the sandwich on a plate.

"So, tell me why you were still in bed on a Sunday morning at eleven am." She gives me a stern look, like she knows what Ive been up to, so I can't help the blush that creeps across my cheeks.

"I've been seeing someone," I admit. It is like second nature to tell my grandma what is going on in my life. It has been weird not talking to her the last few weeks.

"Tell me everything!" she says loudly.

"Her name is Reese, she's my age, still in school but has a job, and I really like her," I say proudly. I know what Grandma wanted to hear when she said everything.

"Show me! Show me!" she says as she chomps away at her sandwich.

I pull out my phone to show her my background. It is a photo the two of us took on one of our date nights where we actually left the apartment. Although that was only because we had run out of food in my apartment and we were closer to a restaurant than to the grocery store.

"She's handsome." She stops. "I can still say that right?"

"Yes, Grandma, that's okay to say." I giggle. She tries hard to keep up with what is appropriate for today's standards. Which doesn't go unnoticed.

"You should bring her around, let me meet her."

"Oh gosh, you're going to grill her aren't you?" I hadn't dated anyone in such a long time that my grandma never had the chance to meet anyone else.

"Yes, because it's only fair I get to know the woman who's dating my granddaughter." She smiles and makes a pouty face at me. I swear the woman is in her seventies but can still make a face and have everyone do what she wants. It is a superpower I hoped to acquire one day.

"Well, I suppose it wouldn't hurt to have you two meet." I shrug.

"Perfect! We should get some bagels from Shelly's so she can try it."

"She's actually already been there with me," I admit shyly.

"You took her there? Wow, she must be special." My grandma knows how much that place means to me and I don't just bring anyone there. She is right, Reese is special.

"Are you sure you want to go?" I ask for the hundredth time.

"Yes, I'm positive. Your grandma wants to meet me, I don't want to stand her up." Reese smiles.

"But you don't have to."

"Babe, do you not want me to?" Reese pauses as we stand in the middle of the sidewalk. I pull her over to the side and sigh.

"I want you to, I've just never had anyone meet her before. It's important to me."

"I'll be on my best behavior," she jokes.

"I'm serious." I frown.

"I am, too, I'm excited to meet her. And I know it's like equivalent of meeting your parents, maybe even more special to you. I'm taking this seriously." Reese leans in to kiss my forehead, and I close my eyes. With a deep breath and her kiss, I instantly feel better. I don't know why I am worrying so much.

We head to Shelly's to pick up the bagels and then head to my grandma's apartment. Reese holds the bagels the whole way and when my grandma opens the door, she greets both of us with a big hug. I know she just can't help herself.

"It's so nice to meet you." Reese smiles and hands her the bag of bagels.

Lucky to be Yours

"It's nice to meet you, too, I've heard only good things." My grandma winks.

"So have I," Reese winks back, and Grandma laughs.

"You can call her Grandma, everyone does."

"I gave up my name a long time ago, I prefer Grandma, or Grandma Adler." She smiles.

"Got it, Grandma."

"So, which embarrassing story about Ellie would you like to hear first?"

"Grandma." I groan while Reese laughs. "Don't ruin this for me."

"Oh, I'm just joking." She shakes her head at me.

"I'd love to hear any stories about Ellie," Reese adds and I shoot her a look.

"Well, she is my favorite grandchild so I don't think I have many embarrassing stories to tell." Grandma laughs.

"I'm your only grandchild," I point out.

"Oh, shush." She waves me off.

We all walk into the kitchen and take a seat at the table. Digging into the bagels, I cut each of them in half and hand them to Grandma and Reese, leaving one on my plate for me. Spreading a good amount of cream cheese on mine, I watch as Reese covers hers in a thin layer of butter. My grandma adds cream cheese to hers, a good thick layer like they give you at the place.

"So, how did you two meet? Ellie doesn't tell me anything."

"Ellie didn't tell you the story?" Reese asks surprised.

"Nope, I guess it didn't come up." I shrug.

"Do you want to tell it?" Reese asks me.

"You can, I've never heard you tell it." I smile.

"Well, we met on St.Patrick's Day last year. She was beautiful, I spotted her across the bar and she was illuminating with her pink hair and beauty. We hit it off, but neither of us were looking for anything serious so we parted ways. But then we ran into each other again and again. Like something out of a movie. Then we didn't see each other for an entire year but ran into each other on St.Patrick's Day this year, and I knew I couldn't let her go this time. So I asked her out right away and we've been together ever since," Reese explains, and I'm smiling like an idiot by the end.

I appreciate how she left out our one night stands for my grandma's sake, but I love hearing her tell our story. I didn't know she was so captivated by me right away, sometimes I wonder what would've happened if I wasn't in love with Bella last year. *Would we have gotten together sooner?* I have to think that everything happens for a reason and we met at the right time for what we both needed.

"That's like something out of a Hallmark movie! You should pitch that to Hallmark for real!" Grandma is obsessed with her Hallmark movie channel.

"I don't know about that, but it's definitely a special story." I smile.

"I'm serious! Or a book! You know someone in publishing, right? You need to pitch that right away," Grandma exclaims.

"You know someone in publishing?" Reese creases her eyebrows.

"Morgan's girlfriend and Bella's girlfriend both work in publishing," I explain.

"Oh." Reese nods.

"You could be making millions!"

"Okay, I think you've been watching too many of those movies." I laugh. Grandma makes a face at me, and I stick out my tongue at her. We are too playful for our own good. She laughs, and Reese shakes her head at us.

I take a large bite of my bagel and my grandma bursts out laughing. I'm about to ask when Reese looks at me and starts laughing too.

"What?" I ask.

"You have some cream cheese on your face, babe," Reese says in between laughter. I'm glad I wasn't still trying to impress her or anything. I pick up my napkin and wipe my face but Reese is still laughing as hard as grandma.

"Come here," Reese leans in and swipes her thumb across my chin, getting the last of the cream cheese off. She looks deep into my eyes and smiles as she wipes it on her napkin.

"Thank you," I whisper. The tension between us is thicker than I am.

"So, Reese, what do you do for work?"

"I work as a barista, but I'm actually back in school to finish my degree. I'm looking to work at a domestic violence shelter," she explains. I notice her jaw tighten as she says it out loud. I know how close she is to this job choice, but she is sure this is something she wants to do. To be able to help others get out of tough situations that she has been in herself.

"Wow, that's admirable. Not everyone can handle a job like that," Grandma adds.

"I just hope I can make a difference in someone's

life, that makes it worth it." Reese smiles. I reach for her hand and feel her relax under my touch.

While Grandma and Reese continue talking about her schooling and job opportunities, I can't help but smile. It is amazing to see two of my favorite people in the world getting along so well. I was nervous about them meeting but for the life of me, I can't remember why anymore. My grandma and I are so similar, it would be out of character for Reese and her to not get along. They laugh at my expense and both love me in different ways. Well, like me. Reese and I aren't in love, yet. Although the idea has crossed my mind.

"Ellie, are you even listening?" Grandma pulls me out of my thoughts, and I laugh.

"Nope," I admit.

"I was just saying how nice it is to see you so happy."

"Thank you." I smile.

"You should know, I've never met any of Ellie's girlfriends. I've asked, but she never brought anyone around. So you should know how special that is." My grandma winks at Reese.

"It's an honor to meet you." Reese smiles hugely. I can tell my grandma's words meant a lot to her.

Chapter 15

Reese

Ellie looks at me with desire as she pushes me against the wall in the elevator of her grandmother's apartment. "I need you." Her lips press against mine and her hands go for my chest. I've never seen her so ravenous for me before.

"As much as I'd love to do you in this elevator, where's this coming from?" I ask, pulling away. Ellie's hands are still on my hips, holding me close to her.

"I just feel like I want to be closer to you," she whispers.

"Oh." I smile. She must be feeling a type of way because of how well it went with her grandmother. "Why don't we take this back to my place so we don't scar anyone living in this building?"

"That's probably a good idea." Ellie blushes and lets go of me but I grab her hands, pulling her into me for one last kiss. A long one that lasts until we hear a throat clearing and realize it's our floor to get off.

"Sorry," I mumble as I pass by an old man holding a

bag of groceries. He doesn't say anything as we make our way out of the building, toward my apartment.

It's a short subway ride to my apartment that Ellie spends teasing me. Unbuttoning her shirt, making her chest more visible and leaving her hand on my inner thigh the whole ride. I am about to make her pay for all the teasing she did. She just doesn't know it yet. I'll have her begging me to make her cum before I even lay a hand on her.

Ellie's hands are all over me the second we step into my apartment. She's tearing off my blouse and I'm unbuttoning her flannel, clothes are flying everywhere as we make our way to my bedroom. I push her down into the bed, climbing on top of her and straddling her thighs. Her delicious and thick thighs. She's almost completely naked, clad in just a matching panty and bralette set. It is green and I wonder if she bought it because that is my favorite color. I'll have to ask her later because right now I need to tease her.

"I want you," she whispers, and I lean in to kiss her. Our lips moving together as one for what seems like forever. I could kiss her until my lips went numb and still want more.

I pull her bralette off over her head and throw it across the room. Taking one breast in my hand, I lean in and start kissing her neck. Sliding my thigh between hers, I can feel how soaked she already is from barely being touched. I love how wet she gets for me. Continuing to kiss her neck, I nibble on the bottom of her ear and moan.

"Oh," Ellie calls out lightly, and I smirk. This is just the beginning.

"Yes, baby?" I whisper in her ear, biting gently.

"Fuck me," she moans out.

"No," I say in her ear with a bite on her neck.

"W-what?" she gasps out.

"Not yet," I say mischievously. She is pushing her core against my thigh but I am pulling away just enough to tease her. Ellie groans at the lack of touch as I get up and look in my drawer. Ellie and I decided one strap on wasn't enough so we happily went back to the store and bought one for my place. It is a lot easier than carrying it back and forth or being disappointed when we are at one place and it is at the other's apartment. That happening once was enough for us to invest in a second. So I put it on and climb back into bed with Ellie who's smiling and starring at it.

"Yes," she says before I can ask anything.

"Good, I'm going to tease you first."

"More?" she whimpers and I nod.

"More."

I slide my body between her legs and lick her inner thighs, placing soft kisses along the edges of her pussy. Her hip bone, her inner thighs, and just above her pubic bone. She is more than ready for me, her pussy glistening and dripping with desire. I bite my bottom lip, reminding myself to tease her first. I lean my head in and lick achingly slow. From clit to her ass, I lick and soak up her juices with my tongue. Sliding in two fingers, I get them nice and wet before pulling them out. I kneel and look at Ellie, putting them toward her, and she opens her mouth wide, sucking off every inch of her from my fingertips.

"I love that," I murmur to myself.

"Please fuck me," she whimpers again, and I shake my head no. I love it when she begs.

"Tell me how bad you want me," I whisper.

"So so bad, I want you close to me." Ellie groans.

I slip in two fingers and smile as she gasps. I use her wetness to coat the strap on, making sure it'll slide in nice and easy for her. I run the tip up toward her clit, rubbing a small circle before running it down her slit. She moans under my touch, practically begging for more. I decide I've been mean enough and give her what she wants.

"Oh, Reese!" She gasps as I enter her without warning, filling her up completely.

"You like that?" I smirk, and she nods. "Good girl." She moans at my words.

I kneel, using my hips to push in and out of her. She puts one leg in the air and I hold on to her thigh for support. Ellie's fingers slip down and I watch as she rubs her clit gently. She's gasping and moaning, her breath getting heavy, and I smile knowing that teasing must've made her closer than I realized. I pull out and Ellie groans.

"Ahh!" she complains, and I move her body on its side, sliding behind her. We've never done it like this before but I am in control now.

"Like this, baby?" I move her leg so I can fuck her lying on our sides. She nods, and I push the strap on back inside her in one swift motion. I can feel her wetness dripping down her thighs.

"Oh! Yes!" She gasps, and I grab on to her breasts. Partly to steady me and partly because I want them in my hands. I buck my hips and continue fucking her, keeping them in a steady motion.

"You feel so good." I run my hand up her thigh and smack her ass lightly.

Lucky to be Yours

"This feels so good," she calls out.

"I love you," I say before I can think twice about it. It slips from my lips and Ellie freezes. For a moment it feels like the world has stopped.

"I- I love you too," she whispers back. I breathe a sigh of relief. I know it is early, but I have never felt like this before with someone else. Even with my exes, it took me a long time to feel like this. Something about Ellie just makes sense and I don't want to hide how I feel about her.

"Now, cum for me, baby," I whisper in her ear. I fuck her a little harder, feeling her hands moving faster on her clit, knowing that means she's getting closer.

"Oh! Right there!" she calls out, and I keep my pace. I want to hear my girl cum for me.

"Be a good girl and cum," I whisper in her ear.

"Reese! Oh my fuck!" Ellie gasps, and I continue moving my hips until she pushes them away. Turning around, she buries herself in the crook of my neck and I wrap my arms around her. Even though she is bigger than me, she loves being the small spoon.

"Did you mean it?" Ellie asks, looking up at me quietly.

"What?"

"Did you mean what you said?"

"When I said I loved you?" I clarify.

"Yeah. Like it wasn't just a heat of the moment thing?" Ellie asks, making sure.

"No, it was real. I do love you."

"I love you too," she whispers, and I kiss her forehead lightly. Her eyes flutter closed after a moment, she is always exhausted after sex.

While Ellie sleeps in my bed, I sneak into the kitchen and look for something to make us for dinner. We usually end up with takeout most nights but I want her to know I can make her a proper dinner. So I scrounge through my cabinets and come up almost empty handed. All I have is some soup, Mac n cheese, and some bacon. I guess I can make some Mac n cheese, I've never heard her turn it down before. Plus I know once she gets up, she'll be starving. Sex and naps always make her extra hungry.

I boil the water and wait in the kitchen, not wanting to set a timer that might wake her. But a few minutes later I hear her stirring away anyway. Finishing up the Mac n cheese, I put it in two bowls and carry it to my bedroom. Ellie's in the process of putting on a t-shirt but she stops when she sees me.

"Ooo, what did you make?" She smiles and eyes the bowls.

"Mac n cheese, it's all I had." I shrug and hand her a bowl.

"This is amazing. Sex and Mac n cheese, what more could I want?" she says happily.

We climb back into my bed, and I grab the remote. "Anything you want to watch?"

"Something funny?"

"Like a comedy? I can probably find one of those." Ellie's digging into the food while I'm searching Netflix for a new comedy.

It's stupid, but something domestic about this makes me smile. Something about the simplicity of just watching a movie together and eating shitty food in my bed makes me happy. I've never had this before, just being happy with the little things. My ex was always wanting to do more or have more and it never seemed like enough. But with Ellie, she is just happy being with me in the small ways that I am happy being with her. It is one of the reasons I love her. She doesn't make me feel any type of way except happy. It is easy and simple just *being* with her. I know I shouldn't compare my exes, they are two totally different people, but it is hard not to with them being so vastly unique. Ellie makes me happy in all the ways my ex made me feel like it was me asking for too much.

So I find us a comedy as Ellie finishes up her Mac n cheese. She cuddles up next to me while I eat mine, and as she laughs, I realize I'm watching her more than the movie. I try to stop, but every time I do, I realize I'm watching her again. She makes it so easy, her laugh so light and how beautiful she is. I've never been the relationship type, or the cuddling, staying over after sex type, but with Ellie, she makes me want it all. She makes me want those things, and all the things I didn't know I could have. Suddenly, it makes me this cheesy, cliche of a romantic person. Almost someone like Mitchell. God, if he knew what I was thinking he'd be laughing and teasing me for all the times I made fun of him.

"You okay?" Ellie asks.

"Yeah, why?" I ask confused, had I said something aloud?

"You're not watching the movie and you seem to be thinking quite hard about something." She smiles.

"I'm thinking about you honestly, and how nice this is. Just a simple night in with my girl." I press my lips to her forehead and she smiles.

"I like this too," she agrees.

"But this movie sucks," I tease. I hadn't been watching much, but the bits I had caught weren't memorable or funny.

"It does, why don't we do something else?" And Ellie climbs into my lap, her lips pressing against mine as the movie becomes an afterthought.

Chapter 16

Ellie

"Eleanor!" I hate it when people use my real name and when my boss, Kira, does it is never a good sign. I wish I would've filled out my job application with my nickname instead.

"Yes, Kira?" I ask with a smile, putting down my designs. I am in my office working on a design for my upcoming contract meeting. It needs to be perfect and ready as soon as possible so it is taking up all of my focus.

"I need you to take care of this for me, Melanie just quit and I don't have anyone to replace her," Kira says with a huff.

"Melanie quit?" She has been here longer than I have and is working her way up. So it must've been pretty bad if she quit in the middle of the work day. She is one of my work best friends, so it will be weird without her here. She is one of the only other stylists who make plus size designs like I do.

"Yes, yes, something about the work environment." Kira waves me off like it's no big deal. "Come with me." I put down my scissors and follow her down the hall to Melanie's office. It is just like mine with the open windows, the desk, and the row of mannequins for us to work on our designs.

"I need this dress finished by tonight, I also need you to wear it." She points to a half finished dress on one of the mannequins. It makes sense that her designs were left behind, they technically belonged to the company since she created them while she still worked here.

"Excuse me?" I ask, confused.

"I'll be frank, now that Melanie's left you're the only plus size woman in the office. I need someone to wear it and give me feedback on it in the morning. Go to a bar or something and see what people think of it. Can I count on you?"

"I mean, I do have contract work coming up that I need to finish." I sigh.

"Perfect, so you have time then. The dress just needs to be sized to you and you're all set!" She claps her hands and leaves the room without a second thought. I hate when Kira puts me on tasks like this without asking, especially since I am the only plus size woman in the office. I almost feel like I am being punished for that now.

I drag the dress off the mannequin and bring it back to my office. At least it is a nice dress, the beading and lace are beautiful, and the colors compliment my skin tone. Melanie would be happy this dress was in my hands and not in the hands of someone who would try to shrink down her sizes. She and I proudly make plus size clothing that doesn't look like your grandmother's wardrobe or hide your curves. I pop it on the mannequin that has my similar size and get to work.

Kira checks on me once an hour, which is way more than I'd like to see her. By the tenth time she visits, I'm fuming. It's like she trusts me enough to get things done for her but doesn't trust me enough to actually see it through. I hate working for her, and mostly love the contract work I am doing, but it isn't like I could've said no to her. She is my boss, and it's not exactly like she even asked.

"Hey, so the Emmerson Contract people are here and they're looking to see your designs for it." The office assistant, Erin, says, knocking on my door. I glance at the clock, it is just after 4pm but I wasn't expecting them until next Tuesday the earliest.

"W-what? They weren't coming until next week." I was so busy working on this dress for Kira that I thought I had more time with my designs.

"They said they made an appointment for today?" Erin looks stressed.

"Hold on." I run over to my desk and pull out my oversized calendar with all my dates and appointments. Fuck, they were due today. *How the hell did I think they were supposed to come next week?*

"I'll come talk to them," I tell Erin, who nods.

It's two women, both of them the Emmersons. They are sisters looking to expand their plus size lines at their store. I was super excited when I heard about this contract that I wanted to jump on it, but my designs are no where close to being done.

"Hi, I'm so sorry for any delay. Is there any way we could move this meeting to next week? I'm afraid a last minute emergency came up and I don't have all the designs finished for you," I say, shaking their hands.

"You don't have anything for us?" One of them scoffs.

"I thought our meeting was next Tuesday so I'm afraid that I don't have them done yet," I explain.

"So you're unprepared and unorganized?" the other says.

"I'm sorry. I will definitely have them all for you next week, if there's no issue moving the meeting." I smile, hoping they'll give me another chance.

"No, I'm sorry. We're not in the habit of working with designers who are unprepared. We're afraid we're not going to move forward with this contract." They both walk out before I can say anything else. And just like that, my shitty day gets worse.

AFTER I'M DONE with the dress for Kira and it meets her approval, I change into it and call Reese. If I have to go make a spectacle of myself after having the world's worst day of work, then I am at least going to bring Reese along. I know just seeing her can make my day even a little bit better. I am going to soak up all the Reese time I can get. We decide to meet at Puzzles because it's our favorite during the week spot. I'm relieved because I know it'll be busy enough there I can get some feedback on this dress but it won't be so crowded like some of the other bars in the city.

On the way there, I miss the subway by ten

seconds and almost fall onto the tracks. It was my own fault, I was walking on the yellow line but my ankle gave out at the last second and almost sent me falling. Clearly the moons are unaligned or in gatorade or something because today is definitely not my day. By the time I make it to Puzzles, I make my way to the bar and don't wait for Reese to order my drink.

"You okay?" Cody, the bartender asks.

"No, I'm having catastrophically the worst possible day," I admit and chug down half of my vodka cranberry. I don't even like them that much but I am having that kind of a day.

"Do you want to talk about it?" Cody asks just as I see Reese walking in.

"Thank you, but no. I just need Reese." I wave her over and a big smile spreads across her face.

"Hey, baby." Reese gives me a hug and a quick kiss.

"Hi." I force a smile, although I am relieved to see her.

"Can I get a beer?" Reese sets down her jacket and asks Cody. He nods and then Reese gives me her full attention. "Okay, tell me everything."

"It was just one of those days where anything that could go wrong, did go wrong. I got yelled at by my boss to finish this dress, which isn't even my design. My work bestie, Melanie, got fired although they said she quit but I don't know if I believe that. Then I lost a contract that I really wanted and then I missed the train coming here and almost fell on the stupid tracks." I sigh.

"Wow, you had a shitty day. I'm so sorry, baby." She rubs my back gently and I try to relax, but it's like all my stress was just bubbling inside me.

"I just wanted to see you, I thought it might make having to be out tonight a little more bearable," I admit.

"Of course, you can always call me. I wasn't doing much tonight anyway. I was going to see Mitchell, but he understood."

"Shit, I forgot that was tonight. I'm sorry." I frown. I didn't mean to take away time from her best friend.

"No, don't be. You needed me and I'm here." She takes my hand in hers and rubs her thumb over mine. I take a deep breath and try to let my shoulders relax a bit.

"My friends want to meet you," I say, changing the subject.

"What? The friends I met last year?" Reese asks, confused.

"Yes, but they said they want to formally meet you now that we're like dating," I say.

"Oh, that's cool. When?" Reese smiles.

"Brunch on Saturday? Morgan and Bella are bringing their girlfriends too."

"You okay with that?" I give her a weird look but realize she must be talking about seeing Bella with Dylan.

"I'm more than okay with it," I reassure her.

"Good." She leans in to kiss my lips when I feel a cold liquid slipping down my back.

"WHAT THE FUCK?!" I spin around on my stool, screaming out. The woman behind me looks like a deer in headlights.

"I'm so sorry, it was an accident," she mumbles.

"YOU SHOULD BE MORE CAREFUL," I scream. Not only am I soaking wet and now freezing from the ice melting in my back, but the dress I am wearing is ruined. There is red liquid puddling on the ground while the dress is a light lavender. It will be stained and I will for sure be on the receiving end of one of Kira's rants.

The woman and her friend quickly run away while Cody hands me a pile of napkins. I'm about to ask Reese if she can help me dry off the back of my dress when I look at her. She's sitting, frozen in her seat with her jaw clenched and her breathing seems off.

"Reese?" *I she okay?*

"I can't do this again," Reese picks up her jacket.

"Wait, where are you going?" I ask.

"I need some air," she mumbles and is out the front door before I can get another word in.

I look after her, confused. Was she that upset about the drink being spilled on me? Then why did she look like she was upset with me? I finish my drink and head to the bathroom, attempting to clean off the wine. I pull the dress over my head and hope no one comes in. It won't be the first time I was half naked in this bathroom, of course last time it was under more fun circumstances.

Blotting and wiping doesn't seem to be doing anything, so I sigh and put the dress back on. Standing under the hand dryer, I dry the dress at least so I'm walking around in a stained and wet dress. It takes a while but finally the dress is dry enough for me to find Reese.

I walk back out and look around for Reese. The bar is emptier than it was before, had I been in the bathroom that long? I don't know if she is still outside or if she came back in. If she had only wanted some air, I would think she'd be back already. Something is up with her but I don't know what. I know I might have overreacted about the wine spilling on me, but you ever have one of those days where it's the straw that broke the camel's back? That was me today. It wasn't about the wine, it wasn't even about the dress and the fact that I'd be yelled at tomorrow, but it was about that being the thing that really sent me over the edge. I just don't know why that made Reese run out.

Chapter 17

Reese

I'm trembling as I leave the bar. Pushing past people on my way out of the bar. My hands are shaking, and my heart feels like it's pounding so hard it's going to jump out of my chest. My skin is clammy and my head is starting to spin. I push the front door open and I feel my vision starting to blur as I walk outside. The cool air hits me and I'm thankful for it. Almost like a bit of relief from the air inside. I keep walking, looking for somewhere to sit, to try and ground myself. Along the side of the bar there's a small alley that would otherwise look sketchy as hell, but right now it's my saving grace. I lean against the brick wall and sink to my feet, putting my head between my legs and trying to force myself to breathe.

A deep breath in. A deep breath out. Repeat.

I can do this. I can get through this. It wasn't even one of my worse panic attacks, but it was bad enough. I hadn't had one in so long, I forgot how they can sneak up on you. My hands stop shaking, but my breathing is still rough and my chest feels like someone's punched a hole in it.

I pull out my phone and immediately drop my location to Mitchell without thinking twice about it. I know Ellie's inside, but right now she's one of the last people I want to see. Mitchell will be able to calm me down and know the right things to say. We have an unspoken rule when one of us drops the other their location we go to them. No questions asked, we'll find out what's wrong when we get there. It's usually Mitchell being too drunk or me needing help from a panic attack, but it's been so long since I've done this. I'm hoping he's around and can check his phone. His apartment isn't too far from here, and I'm sure I could walk there if I need to, but my legs currently feel like lead.

I close my eyes but that's when the flashbacks start. I try to push it away but it's like a movie playing before me and I can't stop it.

The water from the vase spills over the counter and the flowers fall to the ground. The glass shatters everywhere while she screams at me.

'How could you be so stupid? I told you I'm allergic to flowers.'

'I-I thought you said you weren't to these,' I whisper out. I could've sworn these were the kind she smelled at the grocery store last week

'I'm allergic to ALL FLOWERS!' she screams out.

'I'm sorry, I can get you something else.' I try to collect the flowers from the ground but she stops me.

'NO! Our anniversary is ruined and it's all your fault!' She throws her hands in the air and stomps over the glass in her boots.

'I'll clean it up.' I scurry to the ground, hoping to pick up the pieces of glass before she makes it worse.

The memory of my ex and I play in my head over and over. The way she screamed at me, blaming me for everything. The spilling of the water and the spilling of the drink on Ellie must've triggered me into it. I try to breathe through it, one long breath in, one long one out.

"Hey! Reese!" I hear my name being called and I open my eyes to see Mitchell kneeling before me.

"Mitch." I pull him in for a hug, and he knows something is wrong. We aren't the hugging type, but right now I need the comfort that only he can provide.

"Hey, what's going on?" He sits cross legged in front of me, waiting for me to explain.

"I-I had a panic attack."

"I got that much from your SOS. But what triggered it? I thought you were going out with Ellie tonight," he says, confused.

"E-Ellie triggered it," I whisper. I hate that my body responds this way and I am so easily triggered by things I can't control.

"Ellie? What did she do?" He immediately goes into protective mode. Looking around as if she'd suddenly appeared and he'd have a word or two to say to her.

"She yelled at someone for spilling a drink on her. And I know it's probably because she was having a terrible day and she didn't mean to yell, but she did and I panicked and came out here," I explain. I know deep down that Ellie didn't mean it, but it is still hard for me to separate that from what happened.

"Okay, so she yelled and that triggered a memory

for you and you had a panic attack? Are you coming down from it now?" Mitchell asks.

"Kind of." My hands are still trembling and my heart still feels like I got punched in the gut.

"What can I do? Do you want to talk it through or do some deep breaths? I can sit here with you if that's what you need."

"I-I don't know." I appreciate Mitchell giving me options but I can hardly think, let alone choose which coping skill I need right now.

"Okay, then I will sit here with you and we'll breathe together until you tell me to knock it off." He smiles and I laugh lightly. I know why I called him, but it is a nice reminder of how safe Mitchell feels when I need him.

He starts breathing in and out like I was before so I copy him. The deep breaths make my head feel a little bit better and my vision more clear. My hands are still shaking but they are starting to subside and I can breathe a little bit easier. Mitchell takes one of my hands in his and they're just cold enough to almost give me a shock to the system.

"Can you talk about something to distract me?"

"Sure." Mitchell pauses. "So Anthony asked me to move in with him, but I'm not sure what to say."

"Wow, that's huge." My eyes widen. In all my time, I've never known Mitchell to be dating anyone long enough for this question to pop up so I understand his hesitation.

"Yes, and his apartment is *so* nice. But is it too soon? I mean we've been dating less than a year and I don't want to go through all the trouble of moving in with someone only to have to move out when it doesn't work out." He sighs.

"But what if it works?"

"W-what?" He looks at me surprised. I know I wasn't usually the optimistic one, but Ellie is changing me.

"What if it works and you get to live with the person you love. You love him, right?"

"Of course." He nods.

"Then what if it works. I mean he moved to New York to be closer to you. So why not meet him halfway and move in with him?" It seems like a no brainer to me but I know Mitchell tends to overthink things like that.

"You always make things seem so easy when we talk it out." He chuckles. "I guess Anthony and I are moving in together."

"That's so exciting." I smile. For a few moments I'm able to forget I'm sitting outside the bar with my girlfriend inside. My panic attack subsides just enough to keep my breathing steady and my body from reacting further.

"Are you ready to go back inside?" he asks, but I shake my head no. I'm ready to see Ellie yet, I feel too anxious about it and the last thing I want is to set myself off again. I hate having panic attacks but the aftermath is just as bad, it is like they stay with me for hours.

"Okay." He nods.

I'm about to ask him to talk about something else when his attention is caught on something. I look up in his direction and realize it's not something but rather someone. Ellie is headed right this way, and I don't know what to say.

Chapter 18

Ellie

I walk outside looking for Reese, deciding that she has spent enough time outside, 'getting air'. Whatever is going on with her, we should talk about it. I mean, that's what couples do, right? I know I am new to this whole dating thing but it doesn't seem right that she ran out without so much as an explanation. So when I peek around the corner and find Reese and Mitchell sitting on the ground together, I'm relieved. At least Reese hadn't been alone. Of course Mitchell is less than thrilled to see me. The death glares he's shooting at me tell me I did something wrong. Something very wrong.

"Hey, what's going on?" I look between them.

"We just need some time, Ellie," Mitchell says sharply.

"Well, Reese has been out here awhile. I wanted to make sure she was okay."

"She's not," he says angrily. "But she will be, with some time."

"Okay." I pause and look at Reese, who's avoiding

eye contact with me. I don't want to ignore Mitchell, but I want to hear it from her that she wants me to go.

"I'll be inside, whenever you're ready to talk I'll be here." I offer her a half smile.

"It might be longer than today," Reese says, and I realize how much I missed her voice just in this short amount of time.

"O-okay. Well, I'll be inside just in case," I repeat. Just in case she wants to talk to me today, I want to be ready to hear whatever she has to say. I give Reese one last look and sigh before heading back inside.

I find a spot at the bar again but this time Cody serves me a water and gives me a long look. "You sure you don't want to talk about it?"

"You don't want to hear my troubles." I chuckle.

"Come on, I'm a bartender. It's practically in my job description," he jokes.

"I just don't know what I did wrong. I know I overreacted a little bit about the wine spilling on me, but isn't she overreacting right now?"

"Look." He pauses and leans on the bar. "I don't know how much you know. And it's not my story to tell. But give Reese a break."

"What? Why?" *What does he know that I don't?*

"She's been through a lot. With her past, so if she needs a little time just give it to her," he says and suddenly it all clicks.

Reese's Medusa tattoo. Her abusive ex. Why she is reacting like this. It hits me at once, and I've never felt more stupid. Of course she would have such a reaction like this to me yelling at someone. I can't believe I didn't realize sooner. I probably accidentally triggered her or gave her some kind of a panic attack. Now I feel like not only an idiot but a terrible girlfriend. I want to run outside and ask for her forgiveness, but it's probably the last thing she wants right now. Even though it's killing me, I listen to Mitchell and give them their space. I wish it was me she could confide in, but I understand now. Of course she wanted Mitchell, she wanted comfort from someone she loves.

I sip the water Cody gave me and decide to sober up. It isn't like I am drunk, but I want to be clear and levelheaded if/when Reese comes back inside. I don't want to say something stupid and she will need comfort and clearheadedness from me.

I'm sitting at the bar for what feels like forever. I keep watching the door, just in case she comes in. I want her to see me right away. It's not as crowded as it was, not that it ever was, for a Tuesday night. My phone is sitting face up on the bar, sound on just in case she calls me instead of coming in. I don't know what to expect and I don't want to miss any communication from her. If she needs me I am going to be there. I just need to wait for her to need me. Which is the hard part.

I can be there for her, give her the support she needs if she just let me. I understand why she called Mitchell, that is her best friend, practically her brother. But a small twinge of me wishes she leaned on me instead. Of course, I am the one who set her off, so of course she couldn't come to me. I sigh. It is just hard waiting for someone who doesn't want you yet. I will wait at the bar all night if it's what it takes. I just want to know Reese is okay.

Feeling like I had been sitting here for hours, I finally spot Mitchell. He's walking toward the bathrooms alone so I don't stop him, but make a mental note to get his attention on the way out. I keep one eye on the bathrooms, waving him over when I see him come out. Mitchell looks at me confused with furrowed eyebrows but walks over to me.

"You're still here?" he says, surprised.

"Of course."

"But Reese said it might be awhile before she wants to talk," he reminds me.

"I wanted to be here just in case she changed her mind," I explain.

"Huh," he says, slightly impressed.

"Is she all right? Is she still outside?"

"She's better but not great. She just left a minute ago. I offered to take her home but she wanted to be alone."

"Oh." My face falls, realizing she really doesn't want to talk to me tonight.

"Look, I know you didn't mean to but you upset her and I wouldn't be her best friend if I didn't say I'm looking out for her. I know you really like her, but just be more careful in the future. She's not as tough as she seems." He sighs.

"I know, I didn't even realize what I did. But I understand now, I feel like such an idiot. Trust me, it'll never happen again," I reassure him. I know he's being nice, I saw the look Mitchell gave me before. He is looking out for his best friend.

"Good. Just give her space to feel her feelings and she'll come around. This doesn't have to be the end of anything," he says, and it's like my soul takes a deep breath of relief. Part of me was terrified that's what that meant.

"Does this happen often?" I ask.

"No, not in a long time. So just try to be kind with her, not saying you can't be yourself, but it's different dealing with someone with trauma than someone else. She was probably embarrassed that she got so upset about what happened, but she also has gone through a lot," he reminds me.

"I know." I nod.

"No, I know she's told you but you weren't there for it and she's a ton better than she used to be but that girl put Reese through the ringer, it was a miracle when she finally let her go."

"I'm glad she had someone like you to help her through it," I say honestly. I can't imagine what Reese went through, but I know what a difference a good support system makes.

"She might still want me sometimes because it's what's familiar, but that doesn't mean she won't get to a point where she wants you instead."

"I know, I'm okay with that taking some time."

"Huh, well maybe Reese is right about you then." Mitchell smiles and stands.

"I should get going, and you can't wait here all night for her. But give her a little time and she'll come around. I promise." He smiles and I nod. We say our goodbyes and I close out my tab with Cody.

"Heading out?"

"Yeah, Reese left. I'll be back next time with her," I say confidently.

"That's what I want to hear." He chuckles.

"Thanks." I smile. I don't feel happy, but I feel a bit more hopeful than I did a bit ago.

On the way home I decide to call Bella. It's barely after ten pm and I need a friend much like Reese got. I don't want to be alone right now. Bella picks up the phone on the second ring and her low mumble answers.

"Hello?" she asks.

"Hi, Bells," I tease, using my nickname for her.

"Hi Ellie, what's going on?" She knows I don't make a habit of making phone calls. Especially not so late during the week. We are in our late twenties, after ten pm is late to those of us who work a nine to five job.

"Can I come over?"

There's a long pause so I repeat myself.

"I'm actually not home tonight," she says.

"Oh." I sigh.

"Hold on." She puts me on mute and I wait in silence until she comes back. "Dylan said you can come over."

"Oh, that's all right." I'm glad she can't see my face. It's not that I have a problem with Dylan anymore, but it is just weird to vent to my friend with her girlfriend there.

"She'll be in her office doing work, she won't bother us if you need to talk," she says as if reading my mind.

"Okay. Send me her address," I mumble.

"See you soon!" she says a little too cheerfully. She's been dating Dylan long enough but I've only been to her apartment once to bring Bella something last Christmas. I don't fancy myself to spend a lot of time with the girl I once loved and the woman she is dating. My therapist says that's me creating boundaries.

I look at the address and I'm grateful she's a short subway ride downtown. The last thing I want to do was go back to my apartment by myself. It is rare I spend nights there alone but it will feel especially empty without even hearing from Reese. I sigh. If only I had taken a few deep breaths or calmed down before the woman knocked into me. If only I hadn't overreacted. I walk to Dylan's apartment and try to hide how impressed I am. She owns her own brownstone, I don't even need to buzz an apartment number.

"Hey." Bella answers the door in her pajamas; an oversized sweatshirt and a pair of short shorts.

"You can leave your shoes at the door." She points to where there are other shoes lined up. I pop off my boots and line them against the wall. I commend myself for not bothering to check out her ass as she heads up the stairs in front of me. Things like that don't phase me anymore.

"Dylan has a meeting with China or Japan or something that's on opposite time with us. So we can use the tv room." Bella opens the doors to a large room that looks like it belongs in a mansion. A huge tv hangs in the middle of the room over the very beautiful unlit fireplace. There are two white couches facing each other, both with a variety of throw pillows with funny things written on them. I'm not in the mood to laugh so I don't bother reading them all.

"Okay." I nod. I feel uncomfortable, like I am stepping into a stranger's home. I mean I am, but it feels like we are trespassing.

"Do you want to sit?" She takes a spot on the couch and I hesitate. The couches are white and Im sure my dress is dry, but in the off chance it isn't, I don't want to stain Dylan's couch.

"I have a stain on my dress, which is a long story. You don't have a towel or anything do you?"

"Here." She pulls a black blanket out of a basket on

the ground and places it across the couch, then pats. I only partially feel like a puppy following my owner.

"So, tell me about this stain or what happened." Bella pushes back her hair behind her ear and yawns.

I am getting tired too and I still have work in the morning where I am bound to be in trouble for ruining the dress. So I tell Bella about what happened, not sparing any details. She isn't here to judge and I know she won't repeat any of this to Reese. It won't make any sense if I don't tell her every part of it. Of course I'm as vague as possible about Reese's past, that part doesn't need details, it's not mine to tell. She's quiet as I explain everything, nodding or listening intently.

"I just feel like I fucked up and now there's nothing I can do."

"Okay, do you want advice or just for me to listen?" Her and I have always asked this after a venting session. It is our way of making sure we are giving each other what the other needs and not what we think they need.

"Advice, please."

"Okay, you made a mistake, yes. But I don't think this is the end of you both. Sure, I don't know her very well but just from what you've said and what I do know, this girl is clearly in love with you. She needs a little time, but she'll come back around."

"So just wait?"

"Yes, or maybe send her a little text."

"A text?" I look at her, confused. "Saying what?"

"That you are respecting her getting space but you want her to know you're waiting and will be there when she needs you. Sometimes people just need the reassurance that you aren't going anywhere and it can go a long way."

"Huh, that's a good idea."

"I have those from time to time." Bella laughs.

"Do you?" I raise an eyebrow, jokingly.

"Hey!" She smacks me with one of the pillows.

"I wasn't ready!" I pick up a pillow and hit her in the chest with it.

We go back and forth a few times, giggling and hitting each other with the pillows until Dylan runs in.

"What's going on?!" she exclaims. We both go silent like we're getting yelled at by a parent.

"We were, um, having a pillow fight," Bella whispers.

"Thank god, I thought someone was hurt." Dylan laughs and rolls her eyes.

"Nope, just letting out some steam." Bella smiles.

"Well, sorry to interrupt then. My meeting is over, so have fun." Dylan kisses Bella on the head, and I don't even shy away. I don't feel anything, similar to how it is when I see my parents kiss. Just kind of gross and whatever about it. Bella hits me with the pillow again one last time once Dylan's out of the room.

Chapter 19

Ellie

I had taken Bella's advice and sent Reese a text. It was simple, just telling her I loved her and I would wait as long as she needed. I meant it too. I was imagining my life without her, and it was almost impossible. In such a short amount of time, she had wrapped herself around me. I was in love with her and couldn't imagine not being able to be with her. It had only been four days, but I missed her like crazy. Something that rarely happened to me. I kept hoping my phone would ring and it would be Reese, ready to talk about everything. But that never happened. Even my text got a heart reaction but no words back. Not a single text.

I still didn't blame her, and I tried to stay positive. Mitchell and Bella had reassured me, space was temporary. I just wish I knew what this meant to her. I didn't want to have a Ross and Rachel situation where she thinks this is a break or something when it's not. It was like my relationship with Reese was up in the air and I hated every second.

As I get ready for brunch with my friends, I can't help but wonder if Reese was going to show up. She knew it was today, and how important it was to me she re-met my friends. I had even sent her a little reminder text about brunch that she hadn't replied to. I hadn't bothered telling Morgan about what was going on, but if Reese didn't show up today, I would have to. They would be supportive, but it wouldn't be the same without her there. I'd feel like the fifth wheel amongst happy couples. Which was even worse than being a third wheel.

Sighing, I get dressed in my favorite romper and cardigan. Something I had created myself at work. Speaking of work, I was dreading going in tomorrow. Thankfully, Kira had been on a spur-of-the-moment vacation all this week and she hadn't found out about what happened to the dress. Which gave me the perfect time to create a new one from scratch. It was only a tad different, but to someone like Kira who only cared about her own designs, she wouldn't be able to tell the difference. I just hoped I was right and Kira wouldn't give me a hard time about what happened to the other dress. I had kept it in a drawer in my office, just in case she had asked to see it. It was a painful reminder of that night and possibly what I had lost.

It was just after eleven when I get the train. There are no seats, not even one I could squish my ass into, so I hold on to the pole and keep my balance as the train sways gently. Only two stops at the brunch place and a multitude of stairs later, I'm standing outside the restaurant alone. I check my phone for the hundredth time, even turning on and off airplane mode to make sure I didn't miss any calls or texts. I knew I was getting desperate, but what could I say? I was an idiot in love who made a mistake.

"Ellie!" Morgan and Lucy are the first to arrive. Morgan greeting me with a big hug and a smile. Lucy and I were a little more friendly than Dylan and I, so I give her a hug too.

"Dylan and Bella said they're running late so we should grab a table," Lucy says, looking at her phone.

"Okay," I nod. We give the waitress a headcount, including Reese, just in case.

"So, is Noel with his dad this weekend?" I ask as we take our seats at a big round table and booth.

"Yes, he picked him up last night." Lucy smiles.

"Nice." I had never met the guy, and Morgan had had nothing nice to say about him but it was still Noel's dad.

"Can I grab you anything to drink?" The waitress asks.

"Unlimited mimosas for the table," I answer, not bothering to look at the menu.

"Actually, I'll just have a ginger ale." Morgan answers.

"What? No, you're drinking." I shake my head at her. "Mimosas for the entire table." I tell the waitress again.

"I, umm, can't drink." Morgan says and I look at her, confused.

"Are you hungover or something? Why can't you drink?"

Morgan and Lucy share a look before taking each other's hands and smiling.

"I was going to wait until everyone was here, but

I'm pregnant." Morgan says proudly, grinning ear to ear.

"You're what?!" I gasp. There was no hiding my shock, but this was amazing news.

"Just about three months now," she adds.

"Wow!"

"Should I come back?" The waitress adds with an awkward laugh.

"No, mimosas for the table except one ginger ale." I change the order and she nods.

"This is so amazing! I'm so happy for you both!" I slide over to hug them both.

"We're very excited, and so is Noel." Lucy smiles. I can only imagine how excited he must be to finally be getting a little sibling. He was over the moon when Lucy and Morgan got married.

"Ahh, I didn't even know you guys were thinking about kids!" I gush.

"We always wanted to give Noel a sibling, and it just made more sense this way. I'm carrying Lucy's egg so Noel can have a biological sibling." Morgan explains.

"I so love that." I smile. Morgan might have been Noel's stepmom, but it was clear she loved him just as much as any biological mother would.

"Is Reese coming?" Lucy asks, and I clench my jaw instinctively.

"Oh, umm..." I'm about to come up with some kind of excuse why she isn't when Bella's voice carries over to the table.

"Hey!" She's carrying an oversized bag that she kicks under the table before hugging everyone.

"Dylan and I came from my apartment, hence the huge bag." Bella explains.

Lucky to be Yours

"Tell them the news though," Dylan pushes.

"What news?" Lucy raises an eyebrow. It surprised me she didn't already know. I search Bella's hand for a ring, but there was nothing there.

"We're moving in together!" Bella and Dylan say at the same time. They both giggle while we all smile and give our congratulations.

"So no more carrying clothes and enormous bags back and forth." Bella chuckles.

"God, I won't miss that," Dylan muses.

The waitress brings over the pitchers of mimosas and the Champagne glasses for each of us. She places a glass of ginger ale in front of Morgan and Bella gives her a weird look. Then glances my way.

"I thought we were all drinking?" Bella says in an accusatory tone.

"We're pregnant!" Morgan announces, and Bella gasps.

"Oh, my gosh! That's so amazing!" She jumps to hug Morgan and Dylan and Lucy, shake hands as if they aren't best friends. They give off that they both aren't much of the affectionate type.

"So, when do we get to meet this amazing Reese again?" Bellas directs the question at me.

I'm sure my face is like a deer in headlights as I panic for a response. It wasn't like I couldn't tell these people the truth. They were my best friends. And my best friends' partners, who probably knew way too much about my romantic life as it was. I sigh, about to open my mouth when Dylan of all people saves the day.

"Isn't that her now?" She points toward the door and my head whips around like an owl's. Sure enough, there was Reese standing in the place's doorway, looking incredibly out of place as she tried to get the waitress's attention.

Before I can say anything, Bella is waving her over with a big smile. "Reese!"

"Hey guys," Reese looks the same, but different. Her eyebrows are pushed together as she looks stressed, but she forces a smile as she says hello. She makes a point of looking at everyone but me.

It had to be a good sign that she was here, though, *right?* I mean, she wouldn't come just to break up with me in front of all my friends. At least I didn't think she would.

Chapter 20

Reese

I didn't know if I would find myself going to brunch with Ellie and her friends today. To be honest, I didn't expect to even leave the house today. But when that second text from her came in, reminding me that brunch was today. I knew it was time I finally talked to her. There was no use putting off the inevitable, and I missed Ellie more than I wanted to admit.

Sure, she had made a mistake, but that wasn't worth throwing our relationship out over. I just needed a few days to clear my head, and now I was okay. My therapist and I talked about it endlessly and it was more of a reflection of me than of Ellie, and I knew that. So I planned to tell her as long as she'd have me back, I wanted to be with her. Part of me was worried that I took too long. Sure, she had said she'd wait, but was she waiting alone? Was she waiting for me, no matter what? It was a lot to put on someone they had just started dating. But we were more than just a casual romance, weren't we? We'd already said we loved each other after all.

So as I walk into the restaurant, I don't entirely know what to expect, but I'm hoping Ellie gives me a minute to talk about everything. Ideally, before everyone else gets here. But as I look around the crowded room, I realize Ellie and her friends are already drinking and laughing. One of her friends calls me over and although my feet feel like lead with every step, I continue walking.

I greet them with hellos before turning to Ellie. She looks just as beautiful as I remembered. I know it hasn't been that long, but damn; I forgot how breathtaking she was. Her long pink hair was curled to her waist, and she was wearing this cute ass romper that showed off her thick thighs.

"Can we go somewhere to talk for a moment?" I lean in to whisper in Ellie's ear.

"I'll be right back," she announces to the table.

We walk back toward the bathrooms and there's a little booth that's empty, so we stand out of the way and she looks at me. It's the first time she's giving me eye contact, but her face is unreadable. I hate that. I hate that only a few days apart made us feel like strangers. I didn't want to feel that ever again.

"Look, if you're going to break up with me it's kind of lame to do it in front of all my friends," she says suddenly.

"W-what?" I look at her, confused.

"Is that not what you wanted to talk about?" She looks confused now.

"No." I pause. "I was going to thank you."

"For what?" Ellie's face relaxes a bit.

"For giving me space and time the last few days. I'm sure they haven't been easy on you, but it really meant a lot that you respected me enough to give me that."

"Oh," Ellie's shoulders relax.

"I just needed to deal with everything on my own. But I missed you tremendously and I hope you're ready to talk and be together again. But I also understand if you need some time."

"I don't need anymore time. I hated not being able to help or be with you," she whispers.

"I hated it too. But thank you." I take her hand and squeeze it gently.

"I love you," she whispers. I breathe a sigh of relief.

"I love you too," I smile.

I hold out my arms and she falls into them, her hair tickling my face as we hug. She looks at me and I push some pink curls out of her face to see her lips. We kiss quickly, but it quickly turns into a more passionate make out than I was expecting. Then again, this was probably the longest we'd gone without sex. I had to admit every inch of me missed her.

"We should head back before my friends come looking for us," Ellie says, pulling away. I wipe my lips in case any of her lipstick was left behind.

"Okay," I mumble. I wanted to keep kissing her, but I also didn't want to make a poor impression on her friends. I'm sure they already thought of me as the one-night stand Ellie had last St. Patrick's day.

Ellie takes my hand and my fingers curl around hers completely as we walk back to the table. She takes the time to introduce me to everyone, and I shake each of their hands before taking a seat next to Ellie.

"So, when are we all taking that vacation the three of us were supposed to take?" Bella asks.

"What vacation?" Dylan asks, confused.

"Every year Ellie, Bella and I go on vacation somewhere, just the three of us. But I'm thinking this year we should allow partners to come too." Morgan points out.

"Now that we all have one, you mean," Ellie chuckles.

"Well, yes." Morgan laughs.

"I'm down for a vacation." I chime in. I didn't care where we were going, I could see Ellie in a bikini or a parka and I'd still think she was sexy as hell. Although now that I'm picturing it, I want to voice to go somewhere warm.

"We should go somewhere warm," Dylan says, as if reading my mind.

"And not too far," Lucy points out.

"Why not too far?" I ask, confused.

"Oh! You weren't here for the news. Lucy and Morgan are having a baby." Ellie explains, and I didn't blame Lucy. I wouldn't want my partner having my baby out of the country.

"That's awesome, congrats." I smile.

"We also have that work trip coming up," Dylan reminds Lucy.

"We're going to a publishing conference with some of our colleagues."

"Oh yeah, Freya and Harper aren't too happy about having to room together." Lucy makes a face and sips her drink.

"Please, those two fight like cats and dogs, but I've also caught them making eyes at each other. I bet by the end of that trip, they're as happy as Bella and I are."

The waitress interrupts us to take our order, and the conversation gets turned around after that. Morgan and Ellie are talking about baby clothes and how cute it would be if she designed some for her. Bella and Dylan are playing footsie under the table while trying to remain not so obvious. Lucy was quiet, just smiling at her wife, much like I was with Ellie. I didn't blame her. She had everything she could ever want right in front of her. Hell, so did I. Now that I had Ellie back, I was sure I would never let her go again. I wasn't rushing into anything crazy like marriage or something, but I wanted her to know she had me for good.

"We should take a trip somewhere I can see you in a bikini," I whisper in Ellie's ear. She blushes and pushes me away with a light shove.

"Alright, sorry to be the party pooper, but I need a nap." Morgan says with a yawn. We've barely finished eating, but she was the first one done. Lucy following closely behind. While the rest of us were taking turns drinking and eating, the buzz of the mimosas quickly catching up to us. Lucy hands Dylan a fifty-dollar bill to help cover brunch and tip.

"Bye, it was so nice to meet you." Morgan gives me a hug before she leaves with Lucy's hand on her back.

"So, where are you guys moving to? Or are you picking one of your places to live?" Ellie asks looking at Bella and Dylan. I guess I missed that announcement, too.

"We're going to move into Dylan's place because it's so much nicer than my one bedroom," Bella laughs.

"Plus, we wanted more space," Dylan adds.

"Yes, it would be easier to live together when we're not on top of each other all the time."

"Well," Dylan laughs and Bella's eyes go wide as she realizes what she said.

"Anyway!" She shoots Dylan a look. "I'm glad you guys worked things out," she smiles at us. I guess Ellie had confided in her friend about what was going on. It didn't bother me as much as I thought it might.

"Bells." Ellie shoots her a look that could kill.

"No, it's okay. I'm glad we worked things out, too." I take Ellie's hand under the table and rub my thumb over hers. She relaxes under my touch.

The waitress comes over to clear the table and we take the hint to start clearing out. It was getting more and more crowded and there were people waiting for this specific table. Dylan, Bella, Ellie and I say our goodbyes and pay for brunch before starting to head out. Before leaving, Ellie turns to me and says she has to pee. I wait outside the single bathroom for her to finish when the door opens and suddenly she's pulling me inside. Ellie clicks the door locked behind us and presses her lips to mine in a frenzy.

"Whoa, what's happening?" I pull away, confused.

"We're recreating our first meet." She smirks. I take a second, but that's all I need to recall the first time we met, and how hot she was being fucked in the bathroom of Puzzles.

I pull her into me, tugging her cardigan off and throwing it on the hook behind me. She unzips her romper and lets it fall to the ground. She stands before me in the tiniest pink thong and bralette and I'm instantly wet for her. I've never seen a woman sexier than she is. My hands are all over her curves in moments.

Ellie's lips are addictive as she kisses my neck, and I reach for her breasts. She slides her cool hand up my t-shirt and across my chest, making both my nipples hard. I moan as she licks her way from my collarbone to my ear, nibbling gently as I slide my hands down her stomach.

"Touch me," she whispers in my ear like a moan. I can't speak, so I nod. My hands ripping her thong as I slide it down her thighs. I reach for her bare core and it's already soaked for me. God, I loved how fucking wet she got. My two fingers glide over her clit, down her slit, and slide in gracefully as she gasps.

"Oh!" I shush her instinctively. We were still in a restaurant and who knew how sound proof this bathroom was?

"Mmm," she whispers as I begin to move my fingers in and out of her core.

"I want you," I whisper. I move her around, so her back is to me and she can see herself in the mirror as my hands slip around and slide back inside her.

"Fuck," she moans.

"Look at us. Look how sexy you are when you cum." I push some of her hair out of the way and grip her neck so she looks in the mirror as I finger fuck her.

"Oh, Reese," she says my name like a song. A song I only want her to sing to me.

"I want you to cum for me, baby, and it has to be quick." I urge her, pumping my fingers in and out even faster. She slides a hand down her stomach and starts rubbing small circles around her clit.

"I'm so close," she whispers. I kiss her neck, letting

her watch us as I push her closer and closer to an orgasm. I can feel her tightening around my fingers. She begins to have shallow breaths and gasps as she gets closer, so I don't stop as she starts moaning my name. I slap a hand across her mouth and she bites down on my fingers to keep her from screaming too loudly. Watching her cum in the mirror, I can see her fighting to keep her eyes open to watch.

"Well fuck," she says breathing heavily, gripping the sink in front of her.

"That was so sexy." I smile. I kiss her cheek and she leans into me for a moment, letting me hold her close.

"Your turn?" She smirks, and I'm about to say yes when there's a knock at the door.

"Why don't we take this back to your place and we can properly fuck each other?" I suggest.

"Mmm, good. I need some time to recover from that one." She says with a giggle.

Ellie picks up her romper, her thong, and looks at the shreds I left it in. I give her a shrug and she laughs, throwing it away. There's another knock at the door and she hurries up, putting her romper back on, with no panties and her cardigan. I was going to have to keep my hands to myself, but that might be hard knowing she wasn't wearing any panties. I give her one last chaste kiss and wash my hands before we open the door.

A woman pushes her way through before seeing me. She stops in her tracks and looks horrified as she realizes what we were probably doing in here. "Ugh." She makes a disgusted face, which causes Ellie and I to crack up as we leave the bathroom. Nothing was funnier than an old lady catching you doing your girlfriend in a random bathroom.

Epilogue

1 Year Later...

ELLIE

"Are we really doing this?" Reese asks for the tenth time.

"We are," I smile.

"She'll be here any minute. There's no changing our minds now."

"Do you want to?"

"No. I love her already."

"Me too." I add. "Plus, we said it's a sign, her birthday is St. Patrick's day."

"She couldn't be more perfect for us." Reese agrees.

Reese and I decided while our friends were getting engaged and married, us moving in together didn't seem like enough. Now while neither of us wanted to have kids, we wanted to have an apartment full of dogs to come home to. Which is how we started the process of looking to adopt. Rocky was a Bernese Mountain and Australian Shepard mix, and set to come live with us today. Just a few days past her third birthday. Another family had her but they couldn't give her all the attention she needed so they put her up for adoption. Once Reese and I saw her, we knew she was the one for us, then when we saw she was born on St. Patrick's day we took it as a sign from the universe.

"She's here!" Reese says excitedly from the living room window.

We had moved out of our respective apartments a few months ago, settling for a place in midtown. Neither of us had wanted to move into the other's apartment where so many other women had been before. It was hard to leave my apartment behind, but I was closer to Morgan and my job now so I didn't mind that much. Plus Reese was happy since she was closer to her classes.

"Let her in." I laugh. She heads to the front door and I follow close behind. We both got the chance to pet her at the shelter but not enough to bond with her yet. I wanted her to love us both, but I secretly wanted her to love me just a little more.

The woman from the shelter goes over some basic information and gives us a few things of Rocky's from the shelter. We had bought her a fresh bowl, food, lots of toys and a new leash but it was good she had some familiar things with her. She leaves and we take Rocky upstairs to her new home. We give her a few minutes to take everything in, she's not exactly a puppy, and she was house trained so we don't have to worry about her tearing things up.

Reese sits on the ground and I sit across the room, rolling the ball back and forth to each other. Rocky joins in after a few minutes, chewing on it and then giving it to the other. She's so fluffy and cute that I can't help myself and pull her in for a big hug. She doesn't resist, instead licking my face as if to say I love you too.

"She loves you," Reese points out.

"She knows who bought her the cool ball." I wink.

"I bought that." Reese deadpans.

"Shh," I shush her with a laugh.

We play with Rocky until she does a loud yawn bark kind of thing and finds her spot in the kitchen. It's an enormous and comfortable dog bed we tried out, making sure it was the best. She almost nods in approval and then Reese and I look at each other.

"Wanna go have sex until she wants to play again?" Reese asks with a smirk.

"And this is why I love you." I smile. Reese helps me up and we sneak our way into the bedroom with a laugh. Clothes go flying and I never tire of seeing Reese naked. I could only see her naked for the rest of my days and I think I'd be a happy camper.

Reese licks my neck, running her hands over my already hardened nipples. She climbs on top of me, her body pushing against mine in a frenzy. We didn't know how much time we had or if we'd have to stop. It was almost like having a new baby. Reese slides her hand between my legs and starts teasing my core. She knew all the right spots to drive me wild. I grab her ass to pull her closer to me, kissing turning into making out as our bodies grind against each other.

"Fuck," Reese moans into my mouth as I grab her neck, choking her lightly.

"Fuck me," I smirk and she nods.

Reese runs her tongue from my collarbone, done my chest, all around my breasts, and down my stomach to my core. She stops right above my pelvic bone and begins licking lightly. Teasing me and making me squirm for her touch.

"This is my favorite view," I moan, looking at her ass in the air as she takes her first lick on my core. I must be soaked because she's lapping up every inch of me.

Reese licks my pussy, sucking gently on my clit, taking it between her lips and I cry out in pleasure. She feels so fucking good. Sliding in two fingers, she begins fingering me, as she licks my clit, driving me right over the edge.

"Oh, fuck!" I moan out. "Just like that!"

"You taste so fucking good," She murmurs against me.

"Don't stop," I beg. I wanted her to make me cum over and over. I no longer cared about begging, or dominance with Reese. She could take control any day of the week if it meant I was on the receiving end of her tongue.

"Beg for it baby," she whispers.

"Please babe, please fuck me. Make me cum." Her hands don't stop so my words come out jumbled, but she knows what I mean.

"Good girl," I can feel Reese smiling against my thighs and her tongue goes back to work. Licking and taking control of my clit.

"Oh! Yes!" I call out and she doesn't let up.

Continuing with that perfect combination of fingers and tongue, I'm on my way to orgasm land. Which is why I gasp and moaning when suddenly there's a bounce on the bed and I'm being touched by something fluffy. Rocky's jumped on the bed in between us and is growling at Reese while trying to move her away from me.

"Rocky!" Reese calls out and we're both a bundle of laughter.

"I knew she loved me already," I laugh. Reese and I sit up to give our little protector dog some pets.

"I wasn't attacking her! Ellie, tell her you're okay." Reese says because Rocky is still giving Reese a look.

"I'm okay Rocky, we were um playing. And the screaming is part of the game." I laugh.

"She's a dog, she's not stupid." Reese shakes her head.

"I don't want her scared for life! Or running in every time we try to... play." I whisper the last word.

"She probably wants a walk anyway," Reese gets dressed.

"Can I come? We can show her Central Park." I suggest.

"I'd love that." Reese smiles. She leans in to kiss my lips quickly before handing me my t-shirt.

We get redressed and put Rocky on her new leash. She doesn't fight it and seems excited to be going for another walk. Reese holds her leash while I hold her hand and we walk along the street like a little family. *My* little family. It was weird, when I see Morgan, Lucy, and Noel together they just seemed like a perfect family together. There was no doubt that those three belonged together, I wondered if that's what people would think when they saw us together. Because that's how it felt, *complete*. Like with Rocky and whatever dogs we adopt along the way, it just seemed complete.

We walk along for a bit until a record shop catches Reese's eye. "Can we go in?" She asks like a little kid with a candy store.

"Of course," I chuckle. We tie up Rocky's leash

outside and we head inside the shop. It must be fairly new because it's not one that Reese had been in before. She'd been to most of the ones near us at this point.

"Welcome!" An older man greets us with a big stack of records in his hands. He carries them over to the counter and then comes up to us. "Need any help?"

"Nah, we're just looking." Reese says politely.

"Okay. Well, if you need anything, I'll be over here." He smiles and heads back to the work he was doing.

Reese starts carefully pawing through the records in front of her. I knew she wasn't looking for anything in particular, she just liked to look through the records and see if there was anything she wanted for her collection. It had taken over most of our living room, but we spent too many nights dancing to her favorite songs that became mine. Something that was one of my favorite past times.

REESE

I'm looking through the records, with Ellie's eyes on me. I know she finds this boring, but she always indulges my collection. Which is more than appreciated. Plus, I knew she loved when I put a record on and we'd spin around the living room together. Something I'd only done with her. She made me want to try all of those stupid romantic things together.

I keep looking out the big glass window to make sure Rocky is still there. I guess this is how parents feel. Well, maybe not. They can't exactly tie up their children to go into a store for a moment or two. I just mean in the realm of making sure they're okay. Rocky looks

Lucky to be Yours

happy, she's sitting on her back legs just looking around at the people passing her by. No one seems to be bothering her or even paying much attention to her which is a relief.

"Did you find anything?" Ellie comes up behind me and looks over my shoulder at the records.

"Not really." I sigh. Record shopping was usually hit or miss. Sometimes you'd find the one you're looking for and others it was full of those I had or didn't want.

"Oh," she frowns and I nod. Pawing through the last row of records, I don't have much hope but I look, anyway.

Ellie's looking away too, she rarely buys anything but I think she likes to indulge me on my exploration. It's one of the last records I find, but I find an old Sublime album that's signed and has a bunch of songs I like, including Santeria. Which was playing in the bar the first time Ellie and I met.

"Did you find one?" Ellie looks at the record in my hand.

"Yes, but it's expensive." I sigh looking at the price tag. We didn't have the money right now to be buying things we didn't need. I put it back in its spot and look at Ellie.

"Are you ready?" I ask her.

"Yeah," she nods. "Let me go to the bathroom, but you should probably check on Rocky."

"Okay," I kiss her quickly and head outside. Rocky is happy to be untied from the pole and almost has me running after her the second I set her free.

"Come on girl, we have to wait for Ellie." I tell her. She makes a whimpering sound but I give her a look and she licks my leg.

"Ellie will be out in a minute," I say. Looking inside, I can't see Ellie and I'm surprised the place even had a bathroom open to the public. Mostly in the city they'd say they were out of order or they didn't have one. Too many times had I been almost caught short that I knew where most of the clean ones were in Times Square.

When Ellie walks out of the record shop with a smile on her face and a bag in hand, I know she's up to no good.

"Oh El, what did you do?" I ask with a sigh.

"I simply bought my girl another record for her collection." She says proudly and shoves the bag toward me. She reaches down to pat Rocky as she looks up at me.

"You didn't have to do this."

"I know, but it's the only thing you'll let me buy you." She laughs. It was true, I hated her spending her money on me, but when it came to records, it was one of the few things I'd accept.

I open the bag and inside was the Sublime record I had just been looking at. I look down at Ellie and smile, "thank you, baby."

"It was worth it for that smile." She says happily. She stands and I pull her in for an elongated kiss. I could never tire of her lips.

"We should keep walking, Rocky's getting restless." Ellie says pulling away slightly.

"Okay." I nod and take Rocky's leash from her. She's happy we're moving again as we make our way toward Central Park.

We walk toward the park and I think about how much in my life has changed since the day Ellie and I met. I never thought I'd be the type to do a relationship, let alone have a healthy one. But I also couldn't imagine my life without Ellie. It took a lot to get us to where we are. Lots of hours in therapy for me, and lots of understanding from Ellie. It wasn't a simple thing for us to overcome, but now there are months that pass without so much as a panic attack or worry.

Ellie and I talked about getting married and having kids but neither of them seemed like things we wanted. More of something that we'd just be checking off on a list and that didn't sit right with either of us. So we'd have Rocky and eventually get her some companions and live happily together. We might buy a house outside of the city one day, but for now we loved our little apartment. It was the perfect place for holiday parties that Ellie loved throwing and the sex we had all over the place. I didn't care where I was, home was wherever Ellie was.

"What are you thinking about?" Ellie smiles.

"You." I wink.

"Oh stop, you've got that mischievous look in your eye."

"I'm thinking about how we never got to finish this morning, and maybe we should find somewhere in the park to finish." I wiggle my eyebrows at her and she giggles.

"You are something else, Reese."

"Ah, my real name?" I hold my hand to my chest joking as if I've been shot.

"Yes, when you are ridiculous, I use your real name." She rolls her eyes.

"Kiss me."

"What?"

"Ellie, just kiss me right here right now." I say smiling. I stop in my tracks and she freezes, looking around. I know what she's thinking, *was I really suggesting PDA in the middle of the park?* But I was. All I wanted was her lips in mine and I didn't care who saw.

"Okay." She presses her lips to mine. Just like every time in the past year, it feels like I'm walking on air while she kisses me. Our lips dance across each other until Rocky tugs on her leash and we pull apart.

"I love you Reese Williams." Ellie says quietly.

"I love you too El," She takes my hand and we let Rocky lead us through the park. A peaceful day with the girl of my dreams.

Also by Shannon O'Connor

ONLY IN SEASIDE SERIES

(*each book can be read as a standalone*)

Only the Beginning

Only for the Summer

Only for Revenge

Only for the Baby

Only for Convenience

Only for the Holidays

Only for the Weekend

Only to Save You

The Only Reason

ETERNAL PORT VALLEY SERIES

(*each book can be read as a standalone*)

Unexpected Departure

Unexpected Days

ETERNAL PORT VALLEY UNIVERSITY

(*each novella can be read as a standalone*)

Freshman Fever

Out Played

EPU#3

EPU#4

STANDALONES

Electric Love

Butterflies in Paris

All's Fair in Love & Vegas

I Saw Mommy Kissing the Nanny

Lucky to be Yours

ANTHOLOGIES

A Taste Of You

POETRY

For Always

Holding on to Nothing

Say it Everyday

Midnights in a Mustang

Five More Minutes

When Lust Was Enough

Isolation

All of Me

Lost Moments

Cosmic

About the Author

Shannon O'Connor is a twenty-something, bisexual, self-published poet of several books and counting. She released her first novel, *Electric Love* in 2021 and is currently working on a sapphic romance novel set for summer 2022. She is often found in coffee shops, probably writing about someone she shouldn't be.

Heat. Heart. & A Bit of Both.

Check out more work & updates on:
Facebook Group: https://www.facebook.com/groups/shanssquad

Website: https://shanoconnor.com

Printed in Great Britain
by Amazon